THE LIFE AND DEATH PARADE

THE LIFE AND DEATH

PARADE

ELIZA WASS

HYPERION

LOS ANGELES • NEW YORK

First Edition, June 2018

10 9 8 7 6 5 4 3 2 1

FAC-020093-18131

Printed in the United States of America

This book is set in 12.625-pt Adobe Devanagari/Fontspring;
Myriad Pro Semibold/Fontspring; and Mundo Sans Pro/Monotype
Designed by Maria Elias

Library of Congress Cataloging-in-Publication Data
Names: Wass, Eliza, author.
Title: The Life and Death Parade / by Eliza Wass.
Description: First edition. • Los Angeles ; New York : Hyperion, 2018. • Summary: Seventeen-
year-old Kitty, still grieving for her late boyfriend, is sucked into the dark, twisted world of the
Life and Death Parade, a group that explores the veil between life and death.
Identifiers: LCCN 2017036593• ISBN 9781484732526 (hardcover) • ISBN 9781368002448 (ebook)
Subjects: • CYAC: Dead—Fiction. • Occultism—Fiction. • Mediums—Fiction. • Grief—Fiction.
• Orphans—Fiction. • Family life—England—Fiction. • England—Fiction.
Classification: LCC PZ7.1.W39 Lif 2018 • DDC [Fic]—dc23
LC record available at https://lccn.loc.gov/2017036593

Reinforced binding

Visit www.hyperionteens.com

A.W.

PART 1

I have seen death as clean,
As life will ever be,
And now I live to see another day,
Did my Lord just punish me?
The pain of life I will therefore bear,
Upon my weakened shoulders,
And ask my soul,
Where I feel love,
To release me from these rivers of blood.

—Alan Wass

ONE

The Start of Summer party was a fairy-lit affair in the back garden of a historic estate. They had a pony ride for the kids, a lighted shooting range for the teens, and a bar for the adults—so they basically covered all the bases of good, old-fashioned country living. I hid at a table up the lawn away from everything, to stop people asking me to refill their glasses.

"Ah, here you are." Nikki and Macklin appeared, carrying drinks. Nikki set his cane down against the table and flipped a chair around, so he was sitting backward. I had a fundamental inability to understand people who flipped their chairs around, so I blinked at him for a while in confusion as he sipped his peach-colored drink. Macklin took the seat across from him.

"What have you been up to?" I said. "Have you found anyone to bear you a son?" Macklin tugged at his collar and gazed off into the party.

"It's just the usual suspects," Nikki said, stretching back in his chair. "Not that either of us is looking." I avoided Nikki's meaningful look. I hated when boys looked meaningfully at me—I could never figure out what they meant by it.

I scanned the party. Excessive abuse of fairy lights meant you couldn't see the actual stars. All the guests seemed to have been invited for their reluctance to question reality and the unshakable belief that heels could be worn on grass.

Nikki leaned over my shoulder. "Should we just leave?"

"We can't just leave," Macklin said.

"Why not?" Nikki had a hopelessly encouraging smile—curved at the ends so he looked like the Joker's angelic little brother.

"Because we're already here."

"Well, we don't have to stay here," Nikki said, reaching across the table to steal Macklin's drink.

"Dad will be angry if we leave." Macklin adjusted the sprig of white orchid in his coat pocket. His black hair fell over his eyes in a curtain. His style was very dandy-in-distress.

"Dad's always angry," Nikki said, finishing off Macklin's drink. "I think he rather enjoys it. What do you say, Kitty? I have a plan and everything. I'll nick one of the rifles and create a diversion, and you and Macklin can race away on a pony."

I grinned. "And you'll join us in three to five when they let you out of prison?"

"Better make it five to ten. I may need to create a diversion in prison."

I let my eyes drift through the crowd until they landed on Lord and Lady Bramley. I sighed. "It's nearly over. Anyway, I don't think you'd survive prison."

Nikki, sensing the shift in my mood, moved closer to distract me. "I actually came over here to tell you something rather exciting. Remember that party I went to last week? The one with the snakes?"

"The funeral." Macklin wrinkled his nose. "The one you said was actually a funeral."

"Well, she's here." Nikki sat back, like his words should have some great effect on us.

"Who's here?" Macklin said.

"The woman from the party. The psychic, didn't I tell you? She's a sort of legend. Apparently she's never been wrong. I've seen her boat parked up just over the hill"—he pointed—"along the canal. I really wanted to talk to her at the party, but she wasn't doing readings that night."

"Why did you want to talk to her?" I said.

"To know my future. Obviously."

"In your case, darling, it's whatever you want it to be," I said. "I don't know if you're aware, but you were sort of born with everything."

"That's not true," he said, and this time I couldn't avoid catching his meaningful gaze, his backward chair creeping closer. I liked Nikki, but sometimes I felt mean about it. I felt like I shouldn't corroborate a world that gave people like him everything they wanted and people like me nothing more than the opportunity to be another thing that people like him got.

I swallowed and then shrugged. "Go on, then. See the psychic if you want to. Ask her what we're having for supper tomorrow."

Nikki sighed in a long, drawn-out way, like he had actually been holding his breath all evening, and then he dismounted his backward chair. "I'll ask her what we're having for supper this time *next year*. That'll really test her mettle."

• • •

I explored the periphery of the party, chasing a stone wall to where the garden met the canal. I walked the towpath, the thin wisp of a trail along the waterway. The water was murky, but sometimes you could see underneath the surface the things people left behind: a corroded chair, a sparkle of silver that could be a coin or a gum wrapper, an open book—pages spread beneath the rusty, blood-colored water.

"What are you doing?" I felt Nikki's breath over my shoulder.

"I'm trying to figure out if that book is worth rescuing," I said, crouched down above the water. I couldn't make out the title headers.

"Any book is worth rescuing." He sat down on the edge of the canal. Nikki had knee surgery last winter after he fell off a horse during his cowboy phase, and even though he'd recovered, he still carried a Victorian cane. He stabbed it into the water, upsetting the book so it disappeared, buried in a cloud of mulch. "Where did it go?" He bent forward. "*Magic.*" He grinned up at me.

"I thought you were going to the psychic," I said.

"I was, but I got distracted." Nikki very often got distracted.

"By what?"

"There was this very beautiful girl walking along the canal." He offered his elbow so I could help him up.

"Oh yeah, which way did she go?"

His arms circled my waist on the pretense of finding his balance. "It's all right. I've found her." His cane dropped and rolled along the path.

"Nik-ki." My head developed a mind of its own and fell into his chest. "Someone might see us."

"I don't care. I love you. I've always loved you. I don't care what anyone else thinks."

"Of course *you* don't." We were rocking back and forth somehow; it was making me dizzy. Nikki and I had been dancing around something for as long as I could remember, but lately the dance had become tighter, more uncomfortable. Nothing had ever happened between us, but when I looked into his eyes I could see my future: a marriage, a castle on a hill. I could see him buying me flowers after an argument ten years from now. And it wasn't that I didn't want it—I wanted it badly—but it scared me. "You're the one with all the power."

"You're *so* wrong." He removed his hands from my waist, pouted like he was actually the boy who never got what he wanted. "You know, it is rather trying, that you only love me when no one else is around." He bent over to pick up his cane. "I don't mean to be a bore, but I do rather think sometimes—" He stopped, sucking in all his breath. Nikki rarely was anything but impossibly nice to me, which unfortunately often made me treat him worse. I was desperate to know what he really thought.

"What? What do you *rather* think?"

His clear blue eyes looked dead into mine. "That you're actually embarrassed by me."

And I couldn't say anything, because he was right. But it wasn't just him; it was the whole idea of love that embarrassed me. Wouldn't I look stupid, walking arm in arm with Nikki through a party? Wouldn't I look weak and naive, to be with someone who had all the power when I had none?

Nikki kept his eyes down for a while, straightening his coat. "Anyway." He cleared his throat. "The psychic's just up there." He pointed to a canal boat moored on the water. Blue spirit bottles hung along the roof. A paper sign was posted in the window: *Psychic, but only if you BELIEVE it.* "Will you come with me?" Nikki rubbed the back of his neck. "To tell you the truth, I'm sort of scared to go alone."

A lump rose in my throat, because that was exactly what I loved about Nikki. He was never, ever afraid to be vulnerable.

And that made him the bravest person I knew. "Yeah. Of course I'll go with you."

We started along the towpath side by side. I took his hand at the last moment, right before he'd have to drop it to get on the boat. Another paper sign was posted above the deck: *Come in! We're expecting you.*

"Ha." I pointed it out. "I guess she must be the real thing."

"You know, it is okay to believe in something," he said.

"And what exactly am I supposed to believe in?"

He gazed out past the canal, toward the skyline, considering. "You have options: the world, other people, yourself . . ."

I tossed my shoulders. "I don't believe in any of those things."

"Me?" He squeezed my hand.

I swallowed my heart to keep it from overflowing. "All right. I guess I believe in you. But don't tell anyone." I helped him onto the deck and followed him into the boat.

● ● ●

The narrow boat was like a home crammed into a hallway. The furniture was shifted at odd angles to fit. Heavily scented amber bottles lined the walls, rotted fruit hung in net baskets from the ceiling. Along the far wall, a candlelit altar glowed. Stones and crystals interspersed with prescription drugs and FINAL NOTICE bills covered every surface. I had to pile on Nikki to avoid knocking things over. He had no one to help him do the same.

"Bugger." A crash. "Rubbish." Another.

I laughed into his shoulder. "Perhaps you should stop moving."

"Who's there?" a voice called from the back of the boat. She didn't seem to be expecting us, which was already one knock against her.

"Shouldn't you know?" I called back. The boat stank of frankincense and Febreze.

"None of that," Nikki said. "This is terribly serious." Another crash. "Bugger." He called out, "Sorry, we're here to see the Future; is she in?" I punched his shoulder.

The lights snapped on with an electric buzz, spotlighting a woman in the doorway. She had good psychic hair, curled and wild like a poor man's Cassandra. "What are you doing here?"

"Shouldn't you know that as well?"

Nikki elbowed me quiet. "I saw you at that party. Last week. Or the week before. I want to know my future. Am I going to be rich? Still?"

The psychic cocked her hair. "If you've come here to make jokes, you can go out the way you came in."

Nikki's smile dropped. I could almost see it slide down his neck as his throat bobbed. He stepped forward, away from me. "I promise not to joke." I doubted he could keep that promise, but he seemed determined. "And I'll pay you, of course." He pulled out a wad of bills.

She put a hand up. "I don't touch the money."

Nikki set the money on a table painted with a black snake and a white snake twisted together. I wondered what it symbolized. Something about good and evil, maybe.

The psychic slipped easily through the debris and put the kettle on. "Are you sure you want to know?" She jingled when she spun around, although she didn't seem to be wearing jewelry. "You seem, maybe, like the type of person who doesn't want to know. Nothing they tell you can change your future, you understand? The things they will tell you are set in stone."

I opened my mouth to argue, but Nikki spoke first. "I want to know."

The kettle screamed. The psychic poured two cups of tea. "Sit down."

Nikki sat, knocking a raven's skull and two candles to the floor. "Sorry." He set his cane down; it vanished like a chameleon.

"I don't see how things could be set in stone." I put my hand on Nikki's shoulder. "Surely your telling us will effect a change. If he left now, things would turn out differently."

"Who are you?" Her eyebrows were painted on, and they dove down when she looked at me. "Has anyone ever told you that you look like a saint?"

"She looks like a goddess," Nikki countered.

"I'm just his friend."

"Well, *his friend*: he won't leave."

"You don't know that."

"I don't know anything. They know. He will stay. *You* will leave."

I laughed in surprise. "I beg your pardon?"

Nikki pulled me onto his lap, rested his head on my shoulder. "She has to stay. She goes where I go."

"No." The psychic folded her arms.

"Let's just go." I tugged Nikki's arm. His eyes had a blank, mirrorlike quality sometimes, so all I could see was myself looking back. I leaned close, whispered in his ear, "Come on, Nikki. Don't you want to prove her wrong?"

He took my hand, kissed my knuckle. "Why don't you go check Macklin's all right? I don't know how long he can survive outside his new car."

"Nikki, come on, this is silly." I couldn't breathe properly. The scented oils seemed to coat the back of my throat, my tongue, my teeth. The windows were covered with black curtains, like it was always after dark. The wood floors were stained with dirt. If this woman was so good at predicting the future, why didn't she sail down to Ascot and win enough money to hire a cleaner? "Please, let's just go."

He pulled me close, his pleading breath along my neck. "Just let me, Kitty. I know you don't like this sort of thing, but *I* do. It's just words. It's not going to hurt me."

I sighed. "But you'll believe it." Nikki, for all his loveliness, had a dangerous permeability about his brain. Whatever the psychic said, he would believe—not forever, but until the next thing came along—the way he dressed like a cowboy after watching a Western, or walked with a limp when he carried his cane. If she told him something bad, he would believe it. He might even go so far as to make it happen. "It's not real. You know that, right?"

He kissed my cheek, then he lifted me to my feet. "Tell Macklin she predicted I'll get his car in the end."

"Nikki."

The psychic slithered forward. Set the teacups on the table. I sighed and squeezed Nikki's shoulder.

"What a load of rubbish," I muttered, and I left him on the boat.

TWO

Macklin was still at the table, waiting for Nikki to return and give him directions. He had taken out his car keys and was spinning them around his finger.

"The psychic wouldn't let me stay." I took a seat across from him.

"Of course she wouldn't," Macklin said. "That's how those people operate. Much easier to convince someone when they're alone and vulnerable."

"I'm afraid Nikki is going to believe what she says."

"Of course he will."

"What if she says something bad?"

He exhaled slowly. "That's not what they do; they say good things so you come back to them."

"What do you think they're talking about?"

"Knowing Nikki, they're talking about Nikki."

"I don't believe in the future." It was hard to believe in the future when you were a third generation orphan, living with a family your mum once worked for. I knew that I was incredibly lucky the Bramleys had taken me in when my mum died, but my future was beyond the scope of any psychic.

"I'm going to collect classic cars," Macklin said. For his eighteenth birthday, he had been given a 1960 Rolls-Royce Silver Cloud II convertible belonging to his grandfather. It was an insanely rare and expensive car. It also made Nikki insanely jealous, which made it even more valuable to Macklin.

"That's not a job," I said.

"Who said anything about a job?" Macklin made a face.

"I don't understand this obsession with wanting things," I said, raising my voice so he might know I was on my soapbox. "Wanting to be famous or wanting to be rich. Nothing ever lasts. I mean, look at the castle."

Macklin's head popped up. "What are you trying to say?"

I suspected I had gone too far. It wasn't very wise to insult the privilege of a family you lived with, although that rarely seemed to stop me. "It's just that . . . it's too much house for one family. And you have to run tours to make money. Nothing lasts forever, not even Bramley money. You might *have* to get a job one day."

He scoffed. "Don't be ridiculous."

"I want to do something important. I want to make a difference."

"You're quite good at archery." This was what they called the English sense of humor.

"Cheers. But I don't have any immediate plans to join the Hunger Games." I was good at archery, but Macklin had missed my true talent. What I was really good at was losing people. Mum was dead. Dad didn't want to know. I had family in the States, and although the Bramleys had offered to send me there to visit, I was too afraid to go. Afraid that if I did, the Bramleys might suggest I didn't come back.

Macklin scooped up his keys. "I wish he'd hurry up. Everyone's starting to go now." He was right. Whatever spell had held the party captive was starting to dissipate. The air was thinning. People were exchanging kisses good-bye. We were allowed to leave.

Right on cue, Nikki staggered up the hill. He tripped and stumbled. Money fell out of his pockets. Macklin went to pick it up.

"I hope you've had your fun," Macklin called up from the ground.

"I want to go home," Nikki said in a dull zombie voice. He wandered toward the road in a daze.

Macklin and I exchanged glances. Nikki never wanted to go home. "He's having us on." Macklin stuffed the money in his pockets and moved to follow.

Nikki hummed as we crested the hill, something like a funeral march, off-key.

"You're having us on," Macklin said again.

I tried to smile, but my lips wouldn't lift. "You're joking, right, Nikki?"

We climbed into Macklin's car. Nikki lit a cigarette. Macklin ordered Nikki out of the car. We waited for him to smoke it.

"I hate when he does things like this." Macklin drummed his fingers on the steering wheel.

"You don't believe it, anyway."

"No, but it's self-indulgent nonsense. Nikki in a nutshell, matter of fact."

Nikki finished his cigarette and got into the car. We pulled out onto the road. Macklin drove extra flashy because he wanted to annoy Nikki. Still, Nikki didn't say a word.

"Well," Macklin said. "Who ever would have predicted? You've learned to keep your mouth shut."

Nikki's eyes seemed frosted over. My throat tightened. I was afraid of something that I didn't know the name of. We had driven clear of the Hartford Estate and settled into the isolated patches of countryside when Nikki finally broke. "She told me I had no future."

"What?" Macklin said. "Did you pay her?"

"She wouldn't touch the money."

"I'm sure her hands were all over it the moment you left." Macklin whacked the steering wheel. "Unbelievable. You can't pay someone to tell you that you have no future."

"We pay the college."

"Are you having a laugh?" Macklin said. "Did she or did she not say that?"

"She said I had no future, and then she escorted me out. She did apologize."

"I don't believe it! Of all the—" Macklin inhaled through his nose. "I'm going to be contacting someone about this. Certainly there's some sort of watchdog organization."

Nikki laughed. The world was back in order then, dragging along in his wake.

I leaned between them. Nikki had a heat to him. Perhaps it was delirium. Perhaps the psychic had slipped something into his tea. "Did she really say that, Nikki?"

"What does that even mean: *no future*?" Macklin said.

"I suppose it means I'm going to die."

"Don't say that, Nikki." I squeezed his shoulder. "That's not what it means. It doesn't mean anything. It doesn't mean anything because she's made it all up."

His forehead had a cool sheen, like he was sweating out some wicked dream. "Listen, Kitty, if I'm going to die, I'm going to die and that's all there is to it. It happens to everyone. Allegedly."

"It's not funny, Nikki," I said.

"You'll have to take that up with God, my dear." He slumped in his seat. "Look at it this way: you lot don't believe in this sort of thing, so you needn't worry." I felt a slight relief then; maybe Nikki was just trying to prove that we *did* believe.

We drove the rest of the way home in near silence, only broken when Nikki asked if he could have a cigarette in the car. Macklin said, "Over my dead body," but nobody laughed.

We rolled down the final hill and the castle rose cryptlike at the end of the road. The Bramley Castle was known for being a bit of a mess. It had started its life as a domed cathedral, then a fortress was added on around it. There was a Gothic extension and a Victorian wing and a lone, unfinished tower.

It was something to be seen, and it could be; tours were available Monday through Saturday from 9 A.M. to 5 P.M. They were limited to the stately rooms in the castle. When we were younger, Nikki and I would sometimes sneak in and pose like dummies.

Macklin's car pulled around the mammoth fountain, where Adam and Eve were forever having a snake-fetish bath, and alongside the stone steps.

Nikki whacked his forehead as the car pulled to a stop. "Rubbish! I've only left my cane on that bloody boat."

"Well, we're back now," Macklin said. Nikki was always losing things. He had lost, had stolen, or had given away nearly every one of his considerable possessions over his short lifetime. It was a standing joke in the family.

"But it's my cane. I need my cane."

"You don't actually need your cane, do you, Nikki? You were walking perfectly fine when you suddenly decided to have a mental relapse."

"I'm making up for how good I was about not using one when I did need it," Nikki argued.

"The party will be over. I don't fancy traipsing around the canal after dark."

Nikki seized Macklin's elbow. "Please. We have to go back. She lives on a boat. She might not be there tomorrow."

"Nikki, you're always doing this. You need to learn to keep better watch over your things."

"Please, Macklin." Nikki tugged at his arm. "It's my favorite cane ever."

"It's your only cane ever."

"So you're with me?"

"I would think someone who had been told by a psychic they were going to die would be rather more eager to get to bed."

Nikki kicked the floor of the car, which was not a good way to cozy up to Macklin. "I don't want to die in my sleep. I want to die for my cane."

"I wish everyone would stop saying that word." I frowned. "You know I don't like it."

"*Die, die, die.* We might as well keep saying it till it loses its power." Nikki was going into a sulk.

"Well, I've had enough predictions for one day." I shoved the door open.

Nikki was undeterred. "Please, Macklin. You can go back there and demand a refund!"

"If we go back there, she'll be the one dead tonight," Macklin said.

Nikki giggled manically.

I shut the door behind me and walked up the steps as Macklin said, "You can buy another cane. You can buy a bloody hover board."

· · ·

Holiday was perched at the top of the grand staircase. She raced down to meet me. Holiday was the "happy" accident in a family with an heir and a spare, so she was over ten years younger than the rest of us.

"How was it?" she said, gathering up the boy's nightshirt she was wearing. She'd had to miss the party because she was recovering from a cold. "Where's Nikki?"

I looked through the front windows, but the car was gone. "They must have gone to the garage."

"What was it like?"

"Exactly like every other party ever." Holiday huffed, so I elaborated. "There were fairy lights. And Nikki spoke to a psychic." I knew better than to tell her about the pony rides.

"Really? What did the psychic say?"

I felt a chill, like what I already knew had taken me by surprise. "Nothing important."

"I wonder what my future is."

"You will go to bed," I intoned.

Holiday patted me on the shoulder. "That's very good. I'll tell Nikki to go to you next time."

"Good night, Holly."

She scooted down the hall. "Tell Nikki he has to play with me tomorrow. It's not fair always being the one left behind."

I went to the staff kitchen and had a supper of instant oatmeal. Then I sat at the top of the stairs and watched Edgar throw drop cloths over the more impressive statues so they looked like a procession of poorly realized ghosts. I was tired, and my mind was hazy with the day, so the castle softened around the edges.

The Bramley Castle was a magical place to grow up. The fact that it didn't belong to me only made it more appealing. There is a certain romance in distance, in being so close to something but never quite being able to touch it. The way Nikki looked sometimes, like all the secrets of the universe were spinning somewhere in the warm recesses of his magnetic brain . . . I could never quite touch him, I could never quite know what he was thinking, and then he would smile his double-edged smile and I would think I didn't need to know everything, anyway.

The sun set beyond the enormous glass windows, heavy shadows seeped in to fill all the cracks in the universe. My eyelids started to droop, so I pulled myself up and walked down the stairs toward my bedroom.

• • •

I always woke up at three o'clock in the morning. Mum used to say that was the hour when the veil between the real world and the spirit world was thinnest, but it was still pretty thick, in my opinion. That morning, I tried to go back to sleep. I put on the audiobook of *The Power of Now*; Eckhart Tolle's narcotic tones nearly always set me to snooze. Still, my heart raced in my chest. I called it anxiety; Mum would have called it a sign, which only gave me more anxiety.

Eventually, I threw off my covers and got out of bed. I went up the stairs and along the hall. Nikki's door was open. I could see him just inside it, as if he were waiting for me.

"What are you doing up?" I said, coming through the door.

He was sitting in front of his dresser with a candle lit, staring at himself in the mirror. "Hello," he said. His face still wore that spooked expression. I could tell the psychic's prediction had really upset him. He had arranged all the objects on his dresser in a weird pattern around the lit candle.

"You should be in bed," I told him.

"Sorry."

"It's okay. You're not still worrying about what that woman said?"

His smile was hesitant. He was wearing a coat I'd never seen before—dark blue and military. It wasn't unusual for Nikki to acquire other people's clothes, usually by trading them for his more expensive pieces. The clouds parted somewhere, but I only saw it on his hair, where light spread in a halo.

"I wanted to say I'm sorry." I fingered the sharp end of a cracked crystal, resting at the center of his makeshift shrine. "You were right at the party, about . . . You know what you were right about." I spun around to face him. "I do love you. I do want to be with you. But I'm scared."

He was quiet for a while, his expression impossible to read. "Love is a scary thing," he finally said.

"Are you going to bed?" I said. "Because I couldn't sleep and I thought that maybe I could . . ." I had slept in Nikki's bed before, once or twice by accident, sometimes on purpose, always in secret.

"Yes." He got off the chair and climbed stiffly onto his tall canopy bed. I took a deep breath and followed him up. He lay on his back, still in his clothes, with his hands over his heart. I moved in close behind him. I felt his breath catch, shudder through him.

"It's all right, Nikki," I said, to comfort him and myself. "It's not real. No one can see the future." I pressed my nose against his neck, and eventually his breathing steadied and the world dropped away.

It was beautiful and wonderful until I woke to him scream-ing. Not a dignified scream, but a loosened, wild one—the sound of a voice that couldn't hear itself. He was slick with sweat and muttering loud and persistent nonsense, and I couldn't wake him up. I tried and I tried, and I couldn't wake him up.

He was alive. He was there beside me. But he was trapped in a nightmare he couldn't wake up from.

PART 2

I wasn't sure whether it was me
or had I died, But
HONEY, SWEET THING
HONEY, I'M ONLY DREAMING
HONEY, SWEET THING
TUPELO IS NOT WHAT IT SEEMS

—Alan Wass

THREE

Nearly a year later

I crouched inside the private altar in the library, finishing off my schoolwork. I had sat for my GCSEs. I had left school. Now I had to destroy the evidence.

> *Lord and Lady Bramley,*
> *   We are writing out of concern to let you know that Katherine Damice's academic performance has fallen drastically since her mocks last year. We are concerned that Katherine doesn't seem to care. . . .*

Their concerns burned. Ashes to ashes, etc. The flames bit my fingers. I stifled a gasp and released the fireball. It streaked to the floor. Then caught the edge of a seventeenth-century rug. I leapt up, stamped out the flames with my trainers, then I sat down to inspect the damage to my soles.

What Ms. What's-Her-Name, *the concerned*, didn't understand was that my academic performance meant nothing. I was going to die and she was going to die and it all meant nothing. It was a warming thought, although possibly that was because I'd just burned my foot.

Anyway, she needn't have been concerned about the quality of my work. I left most of the questions on my GCSEs blank. On occasion, I was inspired to philosophical discourse, when I wrote engagingly about the futility of life. I didn't think I would get very good marks, but I liked to think that one day, possibly fifty or so years in the future, Ms. Concerned would be on her deathbed when my words would come back to haunt her, and with a last dying gasp she would realize I was right.

My thoughts were interrupted by a chilling scream. I shifted the wooden altar to cover the burn in the rug, then ducked out of the vestry, stumbling on my way down the short wooden steps.

We had all been impressed to believe Holiday was very ill. She had concocted an illness of ever-changing symptoms. Whenever it sensed a cure was closing in, it morphed into something else. Holly had gone through twenty-three different nurses in less than a year, and by the sound of it, twenty-four was on the cards.

I knew better than to expect that anyone would try to rescue her latest victim, so I dragged myself toward the sound. I entered the hallway outside Holiday's bedroom in time to hear her shout, "What are you trying to do, *kill me*? Are you trying to *kill me*?"

Her bedroom door flew open. Her breakfast plate sailed and shattered, expelling guts of limp sausage and spattered eggs. The nurse, Janelle, came next, not thrown, but bouncing against the wall after the plate. The door slammed. Janelle gazed at it as if she'd been chucked off stage mid-production, then stuck up two fingers, then saw me.

"Oh."

"It's all right," I said, flashing my two fingers back. I bent down to pick up the pieces. She wiped her brow and got down beside me.

"I've had enough of this. I didn't sign up to look after Colin Craven."

"Nice reference." I scooped up the eggs with my fingers, then realized that was a mistake. "Anyway, you're doing a fantastic job. I've never seen her so good: *transformative*." The door shook on its hinges.

I passed her the pieces of plate, but thought I'd better keep the egg. She tilted her head, considering me. "How can you stay here?"

It was a funny question: *how*, like it shouldn't be possible. "I grew up here." I wanted to say, *This is my home*, but I didn't believe it. Sometimes I imagined myself leaving, going somewhere far and foreign, only in those dreams I was someone else, and I was clever enough to know that wasn't possible. Wherever I went, what had happened would follow me, the way the moon followed the sun, over every hill and valley in the world.

"But it's so . . . *cursed.*"

I cringed. I hated that word. "It's not cursed. It's a thousand-year-old castle. It's England."

"I just don't see how I'm helping." She lifted the tray and headed toward the kitchen. "It's not that I don't care. I think it's terrible, what's happened to them, but they're all so infected by it. I can't help thinking this isn't the last bad thing that's going to happen here. Holiday and her screaming, the mother in hysterics, the father so angry, and the way that boy drives his car . . ."

"One day at a time. That's what they say, isn't it?"

"Or I could walk away."

"Or you could do both and walk away in one day."

We separated in the hallway. I paused in the bathroom to wash the egg off my hand. I generally avoided the mirror, except to check whether my piercing was infected again. I had done it myself, with the help of a dodgy YouTube video: one hole in my face above my lip. I had also shaved my head, mostly so people would stop touching my hair. And I wore a green men's army jacket every day, so taken together I looked like a radicalized guerilla warrior on the lam. Especially when my piercing was infected.

It was pus-free today, but it had a fetching redness. I left the bathroom and analyzed the area for maximum isolation. I was an orphan and this wasn't a Dickens novel, so when I wasn't putting out fires or poking holes in my face, I was hiding.

I bunkered down in a room filled with Victorian automatons—mainly smoking monkeys that were apparently hilarious to the Victorians, seamlessly combining animal abuse and addiction. It was probably the least popular room in the castle because the automatons were downright creepy—the way they moved and weren't alive, the warped shapes of their monkey faces.

I sat in a wingback chair, just sat in an empty room that felt crowded hoping it would make me feel less alone. I took Nikki's lucky rabbit's foot out of my pocket, untangled the two black ribbons tied to the top. I tried to concentrate on being present, on not falling back into the past, on not wondering where it all went wrong, on not thinking it was somehow my fault.

"Katherine?" Macklin stood in the doorway.

"I'm not here. I'm having an out-of-body experience."

He fussed with the automatons, like he had been assigned to general a toy army. Macklin was interesting to watch, if one were objective about it. While all of us were suffering, he had become exquisitely beautiful. His black hair, which he hadn't cut all year, curled around his snow-white neck. His eyes were vivid green. He looked like Dorian Gray, and his portrait was just as well hidden.

"What are you doing here?" I'd thought the automaton room was outside his limits.

"This is the quickest way to the garage." Of course it was. Macklin's obsession with his car bordered on pathological. When he wasn't driving it, he was repairing it; when he wasn't repairing it, he was cleaning it. He spoke about it so much—and he was often the only one who spoke at all—that I sometimes suspected it was more alive than we were.

He talked about it for a while then, crossing his arms like we had met in a racing pit. I had no idea what he said, but I considered hiring him the next time I couldn't sleep.

I shut my eyes, testing. It took him approximately ten hours to notice. "You know, it's unhealthy to mope around all day."

"It's unhealthy to die." I hadn't meant to say that. Macklin tended to bring out the worst in me.

His eyes flicked over me. "You should get out more."

"What? So I can be more like you?"

"Kitty, stop." I was breathing hard. I didn't know when that happened. "I'm only trying to help."

"I know you are. That's the sad thing." He opened his mouth again, but I put my hand up. "You know, I need you to stop saying things to me, because I can't help saying horrible things back. Sorry."

He struggled to find a way around me, like he couldn't manage all the empty space. I felt close to him then, in a brief, fragile moment that ran featherlike between us before it vanished altogether.

Then I stood and forced my way around him, through all the empty space.

• • •

The cleaners would be working their way through the library now, so I wasn't safe there. I had two choices: I could leave the castle or I could go to a place even the cleaners rarely ventured. And I didn't want to leave, so I went up the stairs slowly, with my head held high. I followed the path to Nikki's room.

I pushed the door open and the past pushed back—still living there, crawling like worms through his shoes, like ashes to dust along his dresser. When I was in Nikki's room and I shut the door behind me, I felt him, not in one single place like he was before, but everywhere. Everywhere at once and like a veil I saw through.

If anyone found me in his room alone, I didn't know what they'd do. This wasn't my home anymore; I knew that. Not the way it was before. But I couldn't leave, couldn't dream of leaving. As if Nikki, being somehow elemental when contained inside his bedroom walls, could return there actually—not as a complex of the spirit but in a single, definable place we called a body, with a mouth and lips and the things necessary to hold.

I moved slowly past his dresser, where everything was arranged exactly as he'd left it—gold chains of jewelry in rows, leather-bound journals of all sizes and colors piled up beside an inkwell pen and a vial of dove's-blood ink, feathers and crystals set in a circle around an antique pillbox holding a pound coin and two heart-shaped stones. I let my fingers hover over his things, as if sifting through their auras. With my other hand, I took out the rabbit's foot and squeezed it in a pulse.

I didn't believe in magic, so why couldn't I touch his things? Why couldn't anyone? Why had we left them there, waiting for him to come back?

I didn't believe in magic. But that didn't mean I didn't need it.

I squeezed Nikki's rabbit foot so hard it shot from my fingers and hopped—still rabbit—beneath the bed. I got down on my stomach. The rug was divided into a sea of dust. I saw the rabbit's foot and beyond it, winking like a last magic trick, was the silver handle of Nikki's cane.

I stretched beyond the rabbit's foot and rescued the cane, pulled it onto my lap, and wiped away the dust. What was it doing under Nikki's bed? Had Nikki been mistaken when he said he forgot it? But it hadn't been in the car with us.

I slid backward until I was propped against the wall, rolled the cane back and forth between my fingers. Nikki had left the cane on the boat. Macklin said he wouldn't go back. And then we separated.

I traced a jagged scratch along the body. When did I see Nikki again? Not until three o'clock that morning, when he was still awake, even more unsettled than he'd been when I left him on the drive. Had they gone back to get it? Why had they never mentioned it? I wanted to ask Nikki, but I couldn't. I would have to ask Macklin—which might make my telling him not to speak to me look slightly insincere.

I inhaled, filling my lungs with Nikki. Then I scooped the rabbit's foot off the floor and used the cane to lift myself to my feet.

• • •

We were all sitting down to supper, all except Nikki. There were three dining rooms in the castle, but we used the smallest one, near the center, surrounded on all sides by doors, thirteen doors in all, looking out into the dark.

No one knew where Nikki was, but we all knew he was in trouble. We could read it on Lord Bramley's face. The room was quiet, except for the occasional scratch of a knife on a plate, usually mine.

The front door crashed open. It was far away so it sounded like an egg cracking.

"That'll be Nikki." Macklin made to stand, but Lord Bramley motioned him down. We heard Nikki's footsteps circle around us, heard the scrape of the antique sword he'd taken to strapping around his waist, ever since the psychic made her non-prediction. Other sounds came in behind, clomping in a familiar four-step pattern.

Macklin recognized them first. "Oh my God."

35

Lord Bramley threw down his napkin. "Oh, if this doesn't take it all." He stormed out. Our eyes crossed across the table: Macklin's, Lady Bramley's, Holly's. We stood as one to follow.

We found Nikki marching, face bewitched, along the perimeter of the castle leading two white and two black horses.

"Oh for God's sake!" Lord Bramley said.

The horse nearest Nikki threw his head in the air, then bolted. Nikki released him without a struggle, and the others followed. The four horses galloped into the library, each ducking his head one after the other. The smell of dirt and warm manure filled the room in their wake. Edgar, the groundsman, and his wife, Aislyn, appeared and scrambled toward the library after the horses.

"We had better get you to bed." Lady Bramley dropped her hand on Holiday's shoulder, but Holly twisted away.

Nikki stood with a hypnotized expression, holding the hilt of the sword like he intended to use it, should anyone approach. Lord Bramley must have noticed because he didn't rage immediately.

"Olivia," he said. "Get Holiday to bed."

"Come along now." Lady Bramley directed Holiday's shoulders.

"You're all going to die," Nikki intoned.

"Nikki!" I scolded. He scowled at me. My stomach turned to dust.

Lady Bramley groped for Holiday, who ducked and raced to Nikki's feet. "Nikki? What are you doing with the horses?"

Edgar returned leading two. Aislyn led two more behind. It was like a funeral procession, those horses crossing Nikki's path.

Nikki trembled, then got down on one knee. He reached up with his hand and brushed Holly's hair back. "This is a way to fight a powerful curse, you see? The white to purify and the black to send it back. Have you ever heard of blood magic?" A metallic ripple as he unsheathed the sword.

"This. Stops. Now." Lord Bramley pounced, ripped the sword away, and threw it across the room. He grabbed Nikki by the scruff of his military coat, shaking him until it tore.

"Father, stop!" Macklin said.

"Get Holiday out of here," Lord Bramley said. This time Lady Bramley scooped her up in her arms and ran. Holiday's screams echoed through the hall.

"Father, please," Macklin said. "He's just having a laugh."

Lord Bramley released Nikki with a jerk. Nikki smiled his extra-sharp smile. "Apologies, old man. Just thought we'd get cracking on the apocalypse."

Lord Bramley slapped Nikki across the face. "This stops now, understood? All this silliness stops now. Take off the coat, the boots, the whole mad lot, and I don't want to see that sword again, or by God I will stick it up your backside." His chest heaved. "What do you think it does for your sister to see you like this? She's eight bloody years old!"

"I'm only trying to help," Nikki said. "You'll see, or perhaps you won't. It happens that fast." He stalked off, feinting toward the sword so Lord Bramley stiffened, then headed down the hallway, humming that obscure funeral march.

FOUR

"I found this mechanic who's an expert in Rollers," Macklin told an apathetic audience over supper that night. "I'm going to take him down over the weekend."

"Take who down?" Lord Bramley said.

"The car."

"Humph. I thought you said 'him,'" Lord Bramley said. "Where is Holiday?" We still clung to supper, that one tradition, from Before. Lady Bramley poked the edges of her salad, and Macklin and even Holiday showed up every night. It was our single concession to each other, the slight nod of recognition that kept us anchored to one thing at least.

"I'll go get her." I was sometimes too eager to appear helpful; it was a consequence of feeling like I didn't belong.

Janelle stood in the hallway, playing on her phone.

"Aren't you even trying?" I said. Janelle raised her eyebrows and I blanched. "Sorry, it's just Lord Bramley, he's insistent we all eat together, like proper prisoners."

"She's gone into one of her little things, you know." Janelle knitted her fingers.

"One of her little things," while sounding cute so packaged in words, was Holiday's attempt to channel Nikki. She took on his posture, worked her squeak of a voice around his poetic boom, and generally terrorized everyone.

I sighed. "Wait here, and I'll drag her out."

I paused inside the door, waiting for my eyes to adjust to the darkness. Holiday's room stank of sweat and rubbing alcohol. It was only when I came all the way in, when the door shut behind me, that I noticed the metallic undercurrent, the bad penny smell.

Holiday's room was a shrine to Nikki, but rather than focus on the sweeter things—his boundless charity or the way he could always laugh at himself—Holiday's shrine worshipped the darker parts. The military coat was there, stiff and blackish. The sword was there, too, bloodied to the hilt. I tripped over Nikki's boots.

Holiday sat with her feet crossed. A black hat was pulled down over her face so she looked like a statue, a shrunken tribute to her brother.

"Hello, Holly," I said.

"I'm not Holly." Her voice had a low twang, but she sounded nothing like Nikki. It irritated me. *If you're going to do it, at least do it right.*

"If you think I'm going to call you Nikki, you've got another think coming." My voice broke on his name. I hated to say it out loud; it was like a spell that no longer worked. "Your presence has been requested at supper."

"I can't. I've got to fight them off." The coat crackled as she shifted. She held the sword so it dangled over the edge of the chair. I almost wished someone had thrown those things away. It was terrible to see them, but no one could get rid of anything that belonged to Nikki, even—or especially—the dark things.

"You can fight them off after you've had something to eat, and if I were you, I'd probably change first."

The sword rose. I sat on the floor. My head spun. There was something sick in everything. I put my face in my hands and tried to remember numbers so I could count them.

A clock ticked somewhere.

"What are you doing?"

"I'm counting to ten. What comes after four?"

"Five." Holiday perched forward. "Are you crying?"

"No, I'm taking a nap."

"On the floor?" She had Nikki's true love of chaos. It wasn't part of her act.

I put my hands down. "I can't take it anymore. I actually can't." My vision crossed and double-crossed. "This is it."

"My doctor would say you're depressed."

"Well, it's a good thing you're not your doctor."

"You've got depression," she determined, toying with the hilt of the bloodstained sword. "And you've got anxiety, and you've got manic and you have PTSD—that's post traumatic stress disorder."

"God, I've been busy."

"Janelle gave me essential oils." She clambered up, abandoning the sword and rifling through her bedside table. She held the vial out. "Here. It's supposed to make you calm."

"I don't want it."

She shook it entrancingly. "It will make you better."

"Perhaps I don't want to be better."

"Oh."

I remembered why I was there. "Do you know what would make me feel better? If you came to supper."

She cocked her head, considering. "Perhaps I will come to supper. But I'll have to wear my coat." She clamped it tight around her.

"Do you want to upset everyone?"

"I want to stay here."

I knew I should debate, but my brain had no solid footing. What did it matter anyway? Lord Bramley wanted her at supper, so she would come to supper.

Perhaps a small, naughty part of me wanted to shake him up, and Macklin, too. Macklin never mentioned Nikki at all, even though he had once been the closest thing to him. Lord Bramley was the same, only ever making opaque allusions to "those problems last year." Once at supper a few months ago, I brought Nikki up by accident, recounting a funny story he'd told, and Lord Bramley interrupted me, saying, "We don't talk about those things," like I'd said something vulgar.

He and Macklin had bewitched themselves, with their stiff upper lips and their *keep calm and carry on*s. Something had to snap. Something had to change.

"All right, but if you bring that sword, you're a monster."

She lifted her chin, to show me she was that brave but could be magnanimous. "Come on, then," she said. "Let's join the parade." I joined quicker than she did.

"She's coming." I hopped onto my chair and grabbed my fork as an alibi.

I heard the weighted dragging sound of that demented coat. Everyone's eyes lifted at once. For a moment Nikki *was* back, we were all back, back to that night with the horses, running around the same track, powered by regret.

Holiday paused inside the door. I dropped my alibi. Deoxygenated blood looked nothing like normal blood—it was black and solid and sticky—and it stuck to the coat in chunks. My jaw dropped. What was I thinking, letting her come to supper dressed like that?

Lord Bramley must have been the most English person on the planet, because he regarded her calmly. She crossed the room. The coat crunched and dragged sickly. Janelle pulled out her chair. Holiday moved to sit.

"Take that thing off and put it away, or I will burn it," Lord Bramley said.

"I'm not taking it off," Holiday said. "It's protecting me."

"Take it off." Lord Bramley's fist hit the table. We all bolted up in our seats.

Lady Bramley sobbed. "Let her wear it! Let her wear it if she wants to; what does it matter?"

"I'm not having this." He folded his arms and set his jaw. "I'm not having this madness again. Take it off or get out."

"I never wanted to come in the first place!" Holiday screamed, slamming the chair against the table so the partridges trembled on their dishes. "I hate you! I hate all of you! So leave me alone!"

She rushed out, tripping when the coat twisted, then splayed out like a flag behind her. Janelle followed at a safe distance.

Lady Bramley tried to swallow her sobs. "Why do you have to . . . be so . . . Why do you have to . . ." And then she raced out the other way.

Macklin manfully picked up his silver. Lord Bramley forced down two forkfuls before he gave in, shoved himself back from the table, and announced, "Oh, hang supper!"

I couldn't have said it better myself.

• • •

I caught Macklin on the stairs leading up to his room. He folded his arms, tossed his hair out of his eyes. "What do you want?"

I moved my hand off his shoulder, shook it out like he might be contagious. "Charming."

"You did ask me not to speak to you." He leaned against the banister with that stiff quality he had, like he'd been asked to pose for a painting before he was crowned prince.

"I was in Nikki's room today—" He flinched like Nikki's name was a weapon. "And I found his cane. The one he left on the psychic's boat."

"Well, obviously he didn't leave it," Macklin snapped.

"But it wasn't in the car with us," I snapped back. "Don't you remember? He asked you to go back and get it."

"We didn't . . . or did we?" He cocked his head.

"Well, which was it?"

"I don't remember. You know, I can't really be bothered to remember every single thing Nikki ever did." A hush fell between us, because the truth was he couldn't be bothered to remember *a* single thing Nikki ever did. "Thinking about it now," he rushed in, like he could make up for it. "Perhaps we did go back." He scratched his nose. "Yes, I think we did." His stance was relaxed, but there was a desperate quality to his eyes—or did I imagine it? The trouble was, I didn't really know Macklin anymore (if I ever had). We had hardly spoken in a year, and we had both moved in opposite directions. He became prettier, more comported and conservative. He always behaved with a seeming faux concern, like a shopkeeper unauthorized to give refunds. Meanwhile I became uglier, more uncomfortable, possibly slightly twisted. We were like fun-house versions of our past selves. And I had no idea how to get back to who I was before. I didn't know if I even wanted to.

I realized that I had to tread carefully so as not to scare him off, but also because ever since Nikki died we all had to be careful with each other. We all had an arsenal of raw nerves to exploit. If Macklin wanted to, he could recite a litany of perfectly good reasons why what had happened was more my fault than anyone else's. And I could do the same to him.

"You went back," I said. "But why didn't you say anything?"

"Why would I?"

"Well, what happened?"

"Nothing." He scratched his nose. "We drove back to the canal. Nikki went to the boat and got his cane."

"Did you go with him?"

"No. I waited in the car."

"How long was he gone?"

"Ugh, *ages*. You know Nikki." He rubbed his eyes. "He was gone for actual hours."

My heart rate spiked. "And you never thought to go get him?"

He tossed his shoulders. "You know what he was like. There was no point trying to drag him away—he'd just drag you in and then you'd never leave." His words had a ring of truth. "I fell asleep at one point."

He started to move up the stairs, but I caught him by the

elbow. "Do you think he was with the psychic that whole time? Did he say anything? What did they talk about?"

"I have no idea," he said, taking back his elbow. "I wasn't there."

"But he was different after that. He was obsessed with curses and magic and . . . She must have taught him. She must have filled his head with all that rubbish."

"What does it matter?" That was one question I hadn't considered.

"What do you mean, *what does it matter*?"

"Well, it's not going to solve anything, is it, Kitty? It's not going to bring Nikki back." He had a point; I knew that. I half believed that if I could figure out what happened to Nikki, I could reverse it. That it wasn't too late. And I knew that wasn't true. I knew it. But I still needed to believe it.

"But what if something happened on that boat?" I pressed.

"So what?" he said, and my bones went cold. "Does that answer your question, Kitty? So bloody what? *It's too late*."

• • •

One afternoon, when we were young, Nikki and I went out to the archery range. Nikki had been barred from using guns because he too often seemed to forget that they were real. I had thought that he would be safer with a bow, but I had thought wrong.

He got distracted on the third arrow and overshot. We both startled at the high-pitched scream. *A tuft of fur jumped up, and Nikki's face dropped.*

I disarmed Nikki before I went out to inspect the damage. He had shot a rabbit, right through the heart. The arrow threaded through so perfectly that the rabbit didn't even twitch.

Nikki locked himself in his room.

"If it weren't for me, he wouldn't be dead! If it weren't for me, he would live forever!"

I said it was an accident. Macklin said we should eat it. Lady Bramley was very sweet, but Nikki only opened the door for his nanny, my mum. I snuck in behind her.

Nikki flung himself across his bed. Mum climbed up with him and Nikki crawled over her like a wounded soldier. He bawled into her lap. "I'm so sorry. I didn't mean to do it. It was an accident."

"There, there," Mum said. "It wasn't an accident to God. It was meant to happen. It was his time." I thought that was a dangerous thing to say. What was to stop me from picking up a gun and shooting them both, then saying it was meant to happen? But Nikki's despair subsided, so I kept my thoughts to myself.

"It isn't fair," Nikki said. "I would die right now if I could bring him back!" Nikki was serious about animals. If anyone spotted a spider, he would make a huge production of escorting it outside, and there were a lot of spiders in a castle.

"There are no accidents," Mum said.

"I mean, there have to be some." They both looked at me, Nikki with his tear-stained face, Mum with her holy calm.

"Everything happens for a reason," Mum said. "The danger, my pet, is in thinking you know what that reason is." She reached into her apron pockets. You could find all sorts in Mum's apron. She kept crystals, matches, candles, blessed oils in glass bottles.

Mum was a real blend of religious fervor. Every morning she prayed to the Seven African Powers, every afternoon she practiced meditation. She always referred to some friend who'd taught her—Anaya who taught her how to pray; Amala who taught her to chant. I had never met any of these people, and yet, in a way, they had raised me. They were the pieces that put together my mum.

She pulled out a ribbon. "This is a black ribbon. It's how you keep the dead with you. We'll take that rabbit's foot—"

"Mum," I said, but Nikki was enraptured. He was obsessed with everything Mum said or did, wanted to practice every tradition, learn every superstition. He was raised Catholic, but when his parents weren't listening, he called himself spirited.

"—and tie it off with the ribbon, and you can always keep him with you. And then he'll never die, because you'll always remember him."

They stuffed the rabbit's foot, blessed it with oils and incense, and Nikki kept it with him. It was the one thing he never lost, until he gave it to me.

When Mum died a few years later, I was going through my things, trying to work out what I could take with me. I was a minor living with a family that wasn't my own. I would have to go somewhere. I thought it would be better to run, before the somewhere was decided for me. I was interrupted by a soft knock on the door, followed by a swift pounding in my rib cage. I was sure it was Lord Bramley; I was sure he'd come to tell me it was my time to go.

Nikki entered, and my heart swelled. He bowed his head, climbed onto the bed. It was clear he'd been crying. He watched me for a while before he said, "What are you doing?"

"I'm just trying to think what I might need."

"For what?"

I bit my lip. "For when I have to leave."

His face paled. "Kitty." He stretched out his hand, beckoned me. "Come here."

There was a photograph in my hand, of all of us on the seaside: Mum, Nikki, Macklin, Holly, and me. It felt glued to me, and I struggled to put it down. It shuddered on the dresser when I finally stepped away.

I slunk toward the bed, climbed up beside him. He put his arm around me, stroked my hair. The affection made me uncomfortable; I felt prickly, untouchable. He spoke into my temple. "Do you remember that day with the rabbit?"

I shoved him away. "You think this was meant to happen?"

His Adam's apple bobbed. He took a deep breath, then turned out the silk lining of his coat and unpinned the rabbit's foot. "I want you to have this."

I knew it was important to him; I knew it was the most important thing he owned, and that was why he wanted me to have it.

I took it dumbly. It seemed to upset him more than it did me.

He wrapped his arms around me and he said, like he knew exactly what I needed to hear, "I've told Dad you have to stay here. I've told Dad, whatever happens, you have to stay with us."

I didn't cry, but I felt pierced. Pierced and threaded to Nikki, who was somehow the only one left pinned to me, the only one to tether me to this cursed and rotting earth.

FIVE

After the catastrophe with Holiday, Lady Bramley stopped coming to supper. She stayed up in her room, all day and all night. I felt partly responsible—and God knows I didn't need anything else to feel responsible for—so one night I went up to her room.

She was watching *Come Dine with Me*, which was funny, seeing as she wouldn't come dine with anyone. "Oh, hello, Kitty." She floated in a cloud of comforters and tissues.

"Hello." I sat down beside her dressing table.

She turned to me during the adverts. "I'm sorry if I've upset you, darling, but I can't seem to see the point of getting out of bed." She drew in her tissue subjects.

"You haven't upset me."

She blew her nose. "It's quite nice when it's dark and I pull the covers over my head. Sometimes I dream of Nikki—I suppose I always dream of Nikki—but sometimes I have nice dreams, and I wake up with my head under the covers and think, in that small moment, that he might still be out there. Does that ever happen to you?" she said. I didn't know what to say. "You were always so nice," she said, like I was dead, too. "Nikki loved you *so much.*"

A lump rose. No one ever said things like that to me. I put my head in my hands. My heartbeat pounded in my ears.

"It's so hard as a mother," she said. "I wish I could know he was all right, that's all. He's my son and it's my job to look after him. Sometimes I think—I know it sounds mad—but sometimes I think I should kill myself, to make sure. What if he's over there and he's scared or alone? What if they're not taking care of him?" Her words, contained in their terror, prickled along my neck. "I sometimes think it makes it harder. Not knowing why it happened. It was such a surprise, wasn't it?" She plucked tissue petals to dab her eyes. "There are so many questions. There are so many things we'll never know. I wonder if we did, would it make things better . . . or worse?" She sighed, shredded the tissues with her fingers. "It's mad to think that it was almost one year ago that we were at the Hartfords' garden party, with not a care in the world. . . ."

My mind rocked and I saw that night, the poster in the window reading, *Come in! We're expecting you.* I had been back to the canal after Nikki died, in the dead of winter. The psychic's boat was gone. I had continued along the towpath, searching for it, until all the boats looked the same, until all the boats were *my* boat, in false names and disguises, until the flat water repeated,

52

You have no future, no future, no future. Nikki's future *was* my future.

But boaters followed seasonal paths. Of course the psychic wouldn't be moored there in the winter. She would be there now.

"Isn't the party tonight?"

"Yes. Of course I told Ellie we wouldn't make it. I can't stand to be around other people. They just don't understand— Are you going somewhere?"

I was on my feet. "Yes, well, I—I think I left a candle burning. I'd better go make sure."

She crinkled her nose. "You're not going to the party, are you?"

"Me? Of course not. You know how I feel about parties."

● ● ●

Mum used to believe that dates had a power. She used to say that if you wanted something, you should wait until a birthday or an anniversary to ask for it. And she didn't mean presents. She meant mystical things—good luck, de-hexing, love.

I tried to avoid Mum's superstitions, but sometimes they got to me. Almost one year ago I was with Nikki at the Hartfords' party with no idea things were going to end so spectacularly, so quickly. In one way that was the first last day, in a series of lasts spiraling smaller and smaller, until the very last day I saw Nikki alive.

In one version of one possible world, that psychic was the hinge his life turned on—or off. What had happened on that boat? Only two people knew, and one was past asking. I needed to ask the psychic what happened. I might not trust her to see Nikki's future, but only she could see his past.

I hurried down Lady Bramley's hallway, toward the entry-way. I paused for a moment at the top of the stairs. Beyond the tall glass windows the sky was actually black—not gray or clouded, not a starry, starry night—but black, like a pupil, like a ribbon, like deoxygenated blood.

I didn't believe in magic, but that didn't mean I couldn't feel it.

• • •

I crossed the darkened grounds, heading toward the low hump of the garage. It stank of gasoline. The cars were lined, deeper and deeper, along the garage. The Silver Cloud was at the far end, glimmering as if lit from within. My fingertips brushed its auto flesh. I broke a sweat.

I didn't have to take Macklin's car. It wasn't any easier to drive than the others—if anything it was harder, and the consequences would be greater if things went wrong. I knew I was being superstitious, but they had driven Macklin's car that night. Nikki would have wanted me to take it. And sometimes doing the things Nikki would want me to do was the only thing

54

that made me feel like he was still there—like he had ever been there at all.

I took the spare keys off the hook, squeezed tight the silver key chain. I stopped shaking the moment I put the key in the ignition. It was like the car was an extension of me—a bigger, stronger extension of me.

It slipped silvery under the night sky. I felt the ground drop from under me. Felt the past rise up, in medieval villages and castles on curling hills. I didn't even have to remember where to turn; it was seamless. It was like the wheels had caught on life's secret track.

If I believed in the afterlife, I would have believed it was Nikki or Mum guiding me there. But I didn't, so I thought it was probably some unconscious part of my brain, some hidden autopilot, and it filled me with this tremendous peace. Almost like being under a spell.

• • •

Looking down on the party from the grassy hill where I'd parked, it seemed entirely possible that it had never stopped, that it had been going steadily since last year. A party for the rest of the world that was bewitched to forever stay the same. The same fairy lights crossed overhead. The same ponies made their dull circuits round the lawn. The same guns fired, followed by the same whoops and cheers.

I traced the edge, hoping to avoid people, but because I never got what I wanted, people didn't avoid me.

"Oh, look!" Lady Hartford called out, lifting a hand at me. "It's the Bramleys' girl." Not *the* Bramley girl, mind, but the one belonging to the Bramleys.

"Lady Hartford," I said, because what I wanted to say wasn't very nice.

She crossed the lawn toward me, her expression dropping as she got closer. I was pierced, bald, and barefoot. I wanted to inform her that she was lucky I had put on jeans that day, because normally I wandered around in pajamas, but I thought that might qualify as an overshare. "It's so nice of you to come. Are Oscar and Olivia here?"

"No. In fact, *I'm* not actually here. I just stopped by to . . ." Speak to the psychic in your backyard. "There was a slight problem with Macklin's car, so I just thought I would pull up and, um, make sure it's sorted."

"I'm not surprised," she said. "It's a lovely car, but I told him those old Rollers are a nightmare to keep running, especially when you're as reckless as he is." She took my arm with the air of comforting me, but her grip was a little firm. "We're all very sorry about you-know-what. We can't quite figure out how it happened?" When someone died, people always needed to know how. Possibly they wanted to rule out their own chances. Possibly they were a bunch of rude, invasive sickos.

I jerked my arm away. "I'm afraid you'll have to take that up with God, my dear," I said, quoting Nikki and rushing down the hill toward the canal before anyone else could stop me.

• • •

The dried leaves crunched beneath my bare feet as I walked along the towpath. A long, narrow boat decorated with blue spirit bottles was settled into the basin, exactly where the psychic's boat had been last year. Was it the same boat? I recognized the spirit bottles, but I had a funny feeling, a heavy sense that something wasn't right.

The name of the boat was painted in big red letters: *LOVE*. I didn't remember that, and wouldn't I have? It glowed there, like it was written just for me. But that was stupid; this couldn't be the same boat. I would have remembered that word. We had inscribed it at the top of Nikki's headstone.

Music spooled out from inside the boat: "Dead Flowers" by the Rolling Stones. It was a song Nikki used to play, over and over, on the record player he kept in his bedroom.

I struggled to catch my breath. Something like an electric shock jiggled my brain. It was too much of a coincidence. I couldn't be hearing it; it couldn't be playing. It had to be some sort of auditory hallucination. I gazed back toward the party, but it was lost behind the swell of the hill. A rush of wind jingled the spirit bottles. The wood creaked as a body moved through the boat. I breathed in so deep that I felt the sky sticking to the back of my throat.

There were decks on either side of the boat for boarding, and thin doors with traditional diamond-shaped windows that glowed yellow. I thought I remembered them, but I needed to see inside.

I rested my hand lightly on the railing. I slid forward. The boat slid back. The canal stretched black under me. And then I crashed into the water.

I kicked toward the surface. My head hit first. Hard. In wild bursts I saw exploding stars. My bare feet waded through the mulch. I thought, randomly, of that open book at the bottom of the canal. Saw myself lined up beside it, with the bits of silver, the corroded chair—forever trapped beneath the surface. My lungs screamed. My nostrils stung. I sensed the boat above me, although I couldn't see it. I swam for what felt like miles away from it, before I broke through the water gasping for breath.

The boat was only a few feet away, which didn't say much for my general fitness. A boy was standing on the deck. Smoke swept bewitchingly from the open door behind him.

I spat lake water, paddling in place. "Are you going to rescue me?"

"Do you need to be rescued?" He waited and when I didn't answer, he sighed and stretched out his hand. I took it, and he pulled me smoothly onto the deck.

I stood shaking in front of him, soaking wet. "Are you here for the party?"

"What party?" He had eyes like pale fish caught in the net of his face. His chest was a jungle of chains: silver stars and crosses and a big golden locket at his throat. A William Blake engraving was tattooed down one side of his bare torso, of a figure slip-sliding through fire. "Do you want dry clothes?" He spoke with an American accent, slightly singed around the edges.

"That would be splendid, old chap." My teeth chattered. He arched an eyebrow. He seemed to see right through me; it was a quality of his X-ray eyes.

He led me onto the boat. It was clear straightway that it wasn't the same boat at all. It was immaculate but also soulless, a floating hotel room with polished wood floors and furniture and no decoration of any sort. He led me through to the bedroom. There was an iron bed with crisp white covers, a record player at the end of its tune, and a joint perched in a spotless ashtray. I peered over him, to see the name of the record. It had no label.

"What's that you were playing?" I asked.

He didn't respond, just rifled through his dresser, tossed me a T-shirt, boxer shorts, and a pair of jeans. "There are towels in there. You can shower, if you want." He wrinkled his nose, plucked up the joint, and left, shutting the door behind him.

It felt strange to suddenly be on a stranger's boat, in a stranger's life, with his sandalwood soaps and shampoos and fresh white towels. I tried not to think about how stupid I had been, going there in the middle of the night without a plan. It was probably a good thing I hadn't found the psychic—what did I plan to do with her? Turn her upside down and shake her until the past fell out of her pockets?

As I turned off the shower, I felt the first twinges of a proper downpour. I swallowed hard. I was not going to cry in front of a stranger. Especially not a shirtless stranger. What if he tried to comfort me? It would look like the cover of an erotica e-book.

The boy's clothes were worn soft, more comfortable than my own. I tried to mimic his professionalism. I would say, *Thank you. I'll bring these back tomorrow. Good night.* And then I would leave.

I groped for the doorknob. My fingers slipped. The door flew open. My wet clothes hit the deck. Nikki's rabbit foot hopped across the floor.

The boy was sitting at a table, smoking his joint like a weary prophet. His eyes seemed to dim when he noticed the rabbit's foot. He plucked it off the floor by the ribbon so it spun in the air between us. "Where did this come from?"

I scooped my clothes off the floor, snatched the rabbit's foot, and stuffed it in my pocket. "A friend. He's dead." It was more information than I needed to share, but sometimes I wielded it like a weapon.

"Did he live around here?"

"No, he lived in a castle."

"Some friend." He expelled smoke from his nose.

"I'm leaving. I mean, thank you, I'm leaving, good-bye. Also I will bring these back tomorrow."

"Keep 'em." He didn't seem interested. I started toward the door, when I saw the snakes—the black snake and the white snake—painted on the table he was sitting at. It was the table, the same table Nikki had sat at when the psychic told him he was going to die.

● ● ●

Holiday, Nikki, and I were in the library. Nikki was ill, although he wouldn't admit it. His skin was lit from within but felt cold to the touch. His eyes went dark sometimes, as if he were looking inward instead of out. Holiday and I tried to attract his attention, to cure him with happiness, the way he did us. Macklin was off someplace in his car.

"Look, Nikki," Holiday said. "He's got a coat like you." Nikki wore that long, dark blue military coat every day, no matter the weather. It was a vintage coat so it already had a musty smell, but the smell was getting so strong you could tell when Nikki was coming, where he'd been.

He wore it then, buried in his favorite chair with his ankles crossed over the footrest in tall military boots. He had decided to go to war one day, although it wasn't quite clear what he was fighting, or who would win.

"Hey, Nikki." He was reading an old journal. I snapped my fingers. "Hey, Nikki, Nikki, Nikki."

"Huh? Yes?" He fluttered his eyelashes and met my eyes.

"Holly was showing you something."

"Oh, right, sure." He scratched his chest and checked with the journal.

"It doesn't matter," Holly said like it very much did.

"I think it does," I said. "Here, give it to me." I took the book and approached him. "What are you reading?" I looked over his shoulder. He was staring at a very rudimentary drawing of two people inside a heart. "Nikki, are you stoned?"

"No. Why? Have you got something?"

"When have I ever had weed?"

"I thought you might be turning over a new leaf."

I scooted him over, sat down beside him. I brushed his cheek. I sometimes felt like I had created Nikki. Not only our relationship but all of him, like he was something I conjured to make me believe I belonged, in this family, in this castle, on this earth. "Look what Holiday found, see?" I held the book open. "It looks like you."

"Not at all; I'm much better looking." He shut the book and set it down beside us. He drifted off again, eyes blank, mouth slightly open.

"You all right, Nikki?" I shook his lapel when he didn't answer.

"What?" A note of irritation.

"You keep drifting off. What are you thinking about?"

"Nothing."

I tugged his lapel. "You know, your jacket smells funny."

"It smells of the canal."

"And mothballs. Why don't you have it dry-cleaned?"

"No. It's protecting me."

"From what?"

He shrugged, and his eyes wandered to the drawing of two people trapped inside a heart.

SIX

I saw a tear land on my finger before I realized I was crying. "This is the boat."

"Excuse me?"

"This is the boat. Where is the psychic?"

"You've lost me."

I searched the boat for clues. Lined up along the bookshelf: *The Book of the Damned*, *Hitler's Jewish Clairvoyant*, and *VooDoo in Haiti*. Jars of oils in the kitchen, a net bag of herbs hanging from the ceiling.

"This is her boat. This is the psychic's boat."

"Maybe you should sit down," he said with that eerie calm.

"Where is she?" I spread my arms.

"I think you might have hit your head."

"Where is the woman who was on this boat last year?"

He took me by the shoulders and directed me firmly onto the chair. "Listen, sweetheart, I think you've got the wrong boat."

"But the snakes!" I pounded on the table. "I remember the

snakes!" I wanted to intimidate him into confession, but instead I burst into tears—head in hands, gasping for breath, rocking myself on the creaky wooden chair. He watched with cold detachment.

Eventually I pulled myself together—arranged my borrowed clothes and reached up to organize my hair—until I remembered it wasn't there anymore. "Sorry. I'm not usually like this." I dragged my breath in. "At the castle, I have to keep things together for everyone. I can't cry."

He shrugged. "Don't worry about it."

"What is this?" I traced the lines of the black snake. "Some sort of symbol? What does it mean?"

"It's the mark of this group I used to belong to, the LDP."

"The Liberal Democrats?"

He smirked. "No. The Life and Death Parade."

A memory stirred. "They throw parties?"

"Well, I wouldn't call them *parties*." He rubbed his neck ruefully.

"What would you call them?"

"Circuses. Charades. Cons. I could go on. . . ."

I kept tracing the snakes, over and over. "A funeral. It was a funeral." His lips twitched. I took a deep breath, reining myself in. "Last year. My friend met her at a funeral last year. She was the one I was looking for when I . . ." I made a diving motion. "She called herself a psychic. She had wild, curly hair. Do you know her?"

"I know a lot of people who call themselves psychics."
I searched his face for clues, but there was nothing there. He
seemed deeply untroubled. Or possibly just really, really stoned.

"Do you know where I can find them, this group?"

"Why?"

"My friend, the one who gave me the rabbit's foot, he came
onto her boat to have his future read. She told him he was going
to die. She was right."

"Ha." He scoffed. "That's a first."

"What do you mean?"

"The Life and Death Parade are a bunch of charlatans. Anyway, I believe we make our own futures, don't you?" He winked
at me like he had read my mind.

I gestured to the oils, the herbs, the stones piled in a box
in the corner. "I recognize this stuff. My mum was a sort of
spiritualist. She traveled all over the world, studying religion." I
turned to him. "What do you use it for?"

"Fun."

A large glass aquarium sat on the windowsill. I recognized
the perforated curve of a snake. I walked over to have a look. I
gently ran my finger along the glass. "He's beautiful." The boy
frowned. "Do you like snakes?"

"It was Emmanuel's." The snake shuddered, scales contract-
ing like an accordion.

"Who's Emmanuel?"

"My boyfriend."

"Where is he?"

"Dead. That snake bit him."

I jumped back. "You're joking." I shook the quivers from my hand.

"You think?" His weird eyes flashed.

I moved away from the aquarium and toward shelves of bottled oils. I read the labels, *Kus Kus* and *Uncrossing* and *Flying Devil*, but most of them were unmarked. "How do they read people's futures, these Life and Death people?"

"They petition saints. They build an altar and pray to the saint of their choice, and if they're blessed, the saint tells them things."

"But how do they *really* do it?"

"Haven't you ever heard that character is destiny? They cold read you. It's easy. Take you, for instance." He steepled his fingers and stretched, like he was preparing to dive in. "You're a people pleaser, although you see yourself as a rebel." He touched the place above his lip where mine was pierced. "You do what you think other people want you to do because you think you don't deserve their love. You don't know where you belong."

His words affected me, but that was only because everything affected me lately. "You could say that about anyone," I said. "It's a total cliché."

He jockeyed forward. "And this boy you lost, he might

not have been the best boy for you, but he was the only person who ever made you feel loved. But then, he made everyone feel loved."

The color was leeched from everything, except his stinging eyes. "How did you know that?"

"I told you." He sat back in his chair. "It's easy."

"But you must have known Nikki. You can't have got all that looking at my bald head."

He cracked his neck and crossed his arms. "You said you couldn't cry, so clearly you're a people pleaser. All people pleasers think they don't deserve love. You called the place you live 'the castle,' so you must not feel like it's home. And as for this Nikki, people who think they're unlovable are never loved by anyone except for those who love everyone.

"The trick to reading people is to take whatever that person says to you and say it back to them without all the little qualifiers and nice words people use to keep themselves safe. Say it with intention, and it'll sound real."

"But it's not real?"

"Who cares, as long as it works?"

Was that what the psychic did to Nikki? Took something he said to her and spit it back to him? Nikki had never been one to make plans for the future; he did what he wanted *today*. At least he had until the psychic saw the future for him. "So, this is what you do for a living?"

"No. I speak to the dead."

I steadied myself on the wall. "What do you mean?"

"Exactly what I said. I'm a medium. I perform séances."

"And how do you do that?"

"Different ways." He set his silver lighter over the snakes on the table and spun it between us.

"How?"

"*Different ways.*" He hunched his shoulders.

"By tricks?"

He shrugged. "There are tricks, sure. Things that mean something to everyone."

"Like what?"

"Flowers." The lighter spun. "People usually leave flowers on a grave before they go to a medium. Or they bring an item belonging to the deceased: jewelry or a key chain or a lucky charm." The rabbit's foot burned in my front pocket. "Or they carry a photograph, more the older generation, the younger one has a screensaver or a profile picture. And the pictures are always the same: everyone's smiling, the sun's out." The picture of us in Cornwall sprung to mind. "And the deceased, you describe them in the most general terms, using opposites. *He was the nicest boy in the world, but he had a naughty streak. He loved everyone, but sometimes he could be so selfish.* And the deceased are always funny and they always have that special laugh." He caught the spinning lighter on the desk without breaking eye contact. His voice dropped to a whisper. "And they always want you to know they love you. And they always want you to know there was nothing you could do."

I felt tied to the table. He was captivating, with his weird eyes and his cool demeanor. I could see how a person could reshape their mind to believe what he said. I could see how a person could.

"People need to explain things, it's how they put up with this bum deal they've been given and carry on living," he said. "They want to believe everything happens for a reason. So they decide what that reason is and then they find evidence. There's evidence for everything. So you feed it to them, you tell them what they want to hear, and they make it true because they want to." He rapped his knuckles on the table.

"But don't you think it's . . . *morally reprehensible*, taking advantage of people in their hour of need?"

"I don't see it that way."

"No, I suppose you wouldn't." My skin felt tight. "I suppose you're like all those charlatans in the Life and Death Parade— you think you're helping people move on, giving them closure, and taking their money, of course."

"A boy's got to make a living."

"You're making a living off the dead."

He shrugged.

"You're very cold."

"That is by necessity. You have no idea what it's like, being torn between two worlds: the world of the living and the world of the dead."

"Of course I do. Any grieving person does." I scanned the bare room: structured and self-contained, soulless. "I think you're lonely." He arched an eyebrow. "I think you're very unhappy."

"If you want to know what a person is, listen to what they say about other people," he hummed.

I smirked. "You're a regular horoscope, aren't you?" I stood up. "I suppose that means when you were reading me, you were really reading you. No wonder you named your boat *Love*." I scooped my clothes off the floor. "Enjoy getting stoned."

"Thanks— Hey!"

I stopped at the door, turned to face him. "What?"

He was still sitting at the table. The aquarium was behind him, and it was hard to decide who was more snakelike. His lip twitched. "I didn't catch your name."

"It's Kitty."

"As in cat?"

"As in Katherine. Damice."

His face cracked into an ear-to-ear smile. It didn't seem to belong on his face. "You're kidding."

"What do you mean?"

He clucked his tongue. "You lied to me."

"I never."

"In your pocket." He drew the lighter down the table. "That rabbit's foot came from Darlene Damice."

"Darlene Damice was my mum."

His eyes narrowed. "Darlene Damice was one of us."

• • •

I found Nikki in my bedroom. He'd dragged a box of Mum's things out of my closet. He was using a bundle of burning sage to draw a circle on my floor.

"What are you doing?" I said, aghast.

"I'm drawing a protection circle," he said, like that was obvious.

"You're burning a protection circle. Into historic wood floors."

Nikki blew his hair out of his eyes. "I don't think the floor's history will affect the spell," he said thoughtfully.

"What spell? Why are you putting a spell on my bedroom?"

"To protect you." He sat back, gazed up at me with manic eyes through wisps of pale hair.

"Is this because of the psychic?" I said, picking up Mum's things from the floor and placing them back in the box. "Is this because of what she said? Nikki, I told you: it's not real."

"I'm supposed to be dead," he maintained, running his fingers along the cover of my mum's book.

"No, you're not."

"I'm supposed to be dead, and all of you, everyone in this house, is in danger." He breathed in and got back to work.

"Stop. Nikki, stop." When he didn't, I got down beside him, forced the sage from his fingers. He glared at me. I tried to laugh, tried to act like it wasn't serious. I put the sage back in the box. "D'you know what your dad will say when he sees this in my room? He'll think I've spent too much time at Stonehenge. I'm going to have to find a rug or something to cover it up."

Nikki shook his head. "You have much bigger things to worry about."

"Like what?" He shuddered. He went to pick Mum's book off the floor. "Leave it, Nikki," I directed. He frowned at me. "I don't understand why you're doing this. I don't understand what you're doing."

"I'm not asking you to understand." He set his jaw. "I'm asking you to trust me."

"Nikki," I scolded. "Hasn't anyone ever told you that you have to ask before you draw the sign of the beast in a girl's bedroom?"

"It's not the sign of the beast," he said seriously. He never joked anymore, which was probably the most unsettling thing about him.

"I wish Mum were here," I said quietly. Mum would know, the way she'd always seemed to know, the best way to deal with Nikki. But I wasn't her. I didn't know anything about the mystical side of her. I never thought that one day I would need to fight madness with madness.

"So do I." Nikki got to his feet, left me in the half moon of his protection circle, trapped on the other side of belief.

SEVEN

I started down the towpath, then stopped and stood swaying on my feet. I sat down on the grass. I was in almost the same spot as we were that day, with the canal curved in a basin before me, the boat cupped in an enormous hand. Unexpectedly, I wished Macklin were there. And then I wished Nikki were there. I wanted to cry but I couldn't—I suppose it wasn't inconvenient enough.

Inside the boat, the record player started up again. This time it played "A Whiter Shade of Pale," another fairly obscure song Nikki used to listen to. It was unnerving, but was it that much of a coincidence? They both had record players. They both played songs from the sixties and seventies, when records were at their most popular. Completely explainable. But what about everything else?

The psychic and this boy had both been part of this Life and Death group. According to the boy, so was Mum. But why had she never mentioned it to me? I would have thought the boy was mistaken, but he knew her name, recognized the rabbit's foot.

I took the charm out, held it up in the moonlight like it might offer some clue. I knew Mum was spiritual and superstitious, and she'd often referred to friends I never met, but I had assumed they were people she met when she traveled the world. I had never suspected they might be closer to home. I wondered if the Bramleys knew—but then it didn't seem like something Mum would put on her CV. What was it anyway, the Life and Death Parade? A group of people who went around celebrating funerals and telling teenage boys they were destined to die. A group of people I had to find.

I lay back on the grass, set the rabbit's foot on the apex of my rib cage. There weren't any stars in the sky. I wasn't sure why; there wasn't a cloud, but the sky was black.

I shut my eyes and considered the castle, blessed by the clarity of distance. Maybe if I found this psychic, maybe if I found out what happened that night, maybe if all of us had some answers beyond *it was an accident, but it was meant to happen,* things would be easier. But how could I get the boy to help me find her? I needed him to trust me. But first, I needed to make sure he didn't leave.

I could bring him to the castle. I could hire him as a medium. I didn't think Macklin or Lord Bramley would fancy it, but Lady Bramley and Holiday might. After all, Lady Bramley had told me she wished there were a way she could make sure Nikki was all right.

Exhaustion settled in my limbs, and I rolled onto my side. I would sleep on it. I shouldn't make any hasty decisions. I should run, I thought, but that didn't make any sense. It made more sense to sleep. It was very, very late. Grass blades tickled my arms. Another song I recognized started to play.

*   *   *

I opened my eyes as a shadow crossed the sun. The boy was standing over me, amusement tugging his lips. "Rough night?"

I scrambled up, then shaded my eyes and peered at him. "Don't you ever wear a shirt?"

"Not even to church."

"Amen to that," I joked. He seemed suspicious of my good humor. I should have warned him I made jokes when I felt uncomfortable, which was all the time.

He scanned the deserted canal side. "What are you doing out here?"

The rabbit's foot had rolled off my chest. I picked it up and squeezed it. "I wanted to ask you something. A couple things, actually." I stood up, wiped the grass from my elbows.

"Shoot," he said. He didn't make as much sense in daylight. The sun revealed his unhealthy pallor, the lankness of his hair. The shield of jewelry that hung from his neck was rusted. His eyes were so pale they looked like they were being erased.

"When you perform a séance, does it actually help?"

He shrugged. "It's kind of a mixed bag."

"What do you mean?"

"I mean, sometimes it helps. Sometimes . . ."

I leaned in. "Sometimes what?"

"Sometimes it completely destroys people's lives."

"But sometimes it helps?" I thought that was the more salient point.

"Yeah. This might surprise you, but some people are actually happier after they talk to me."

I rolled the rabbit's foot around my fingers. "It's Nikki's family. Especially his mum and his little sister. I think they'd believe you. I think it might help them. And they'd pay you loads. They're very wealthy."

His eyes seemed to sharpen when I said that. "Are they the ones with the castle?"

"Yes."

"What is it: Mummy, Daddy, little sister, and you?"

"And Macklin, Nikki's brother. But he won't be interested. Neither will Nikki's dad. In fact, I should warn you." I stuffed the rabbit's foot in my pocket. "They probably won't be happy to have you there."

"Don't worry about me. I'm good at getting people to like me."

"Modest, too."

"You came back. Actually, you never left." He winked at me, made a clicking sound with his tongue. "Let me put a few things together."

I followed him onto the boat. Light flooded in from the windows, giving the space an oddly drained quality. Everything around the boy had a strange emptiness—the boat and starless sky and his odd, colorless eyes. He scooped a doctor's bag up from the floor and started to fill it, with crystals and candles, boxers and T-shirts, a handmade spell book.

"What's your name?" I perched on a window seat.

"Roan."

"Roan?"

"It's the color of a cow. I'm the other guy who was born in a manger." I laughed, but he didn't.

"And the Life and Death Parade, what exactly is it?"

He plucked a crow's skull from inside a drawer and considered it before tossing it into the bag. "What is it actually or what is it supposed to be?"

"Both."

"Well." He shut the bag. "It's *actually* a traveling carnival and a shameless money grab. It started out as a religious practice, focused on bridging the gap between this world and the next via saints from all world religions. It's rooted in real traditions and ritual magic from *A* to *Zulu*." His tattoo lengthened as he stretched down to retrieve the bag. "But now you can buy the traditions, you can collect the spells, you can even buy saints and trade them like Pokémon cards. It's kind of like voodoo in New Orleans, or every religion ever: it was great until people heard about it."

"And you have no idea where they are?"

"Not right this second. But they pass through here every summer. They'll probably be here in a few weeks." Great. I just needed to keep track of him until then.

"Is that everything?" I asked. He shook his head and pointed to the aquarium.

• • •

Roan whistled when he saw Macklin's car. He set the aquarium in the backseat, strapping it down with a seatbelt.

"He looks quite cozy," I said.

He sucked the tip of his finger, then ran it along the body of the car. "Killer." He hopped into the front seat as I started the engine.

We sailed through the countryside in bright sunshine. We chatted about the places he'd been: New Orleans and New York and New Haven—a lot of New places. I was sort of jealous. Next to him I had done nothing, been nowhere. The farthest I'd been from the castle was a holiday in Cornwall. I was sixteen years old, and all I had ever done was stay in a place where I felt like I didn't belong.

I drove fast, pulled by the past. I felt like I was going back to Nikki, or at least the pieces of him I recognized. The air tightened, seemed to darken—define itself—around the edges. We were getting close. We crested the final hill.

The castle was far from everything—from the pastoral hills

and the medieval towns that sliced into them like silver scars. When it finally appeared, it was at a dream's distance. There was an illusory stretch where the castle seemed not to get any closer. It happened every time, yet it always struck me as magical, the way the castle maintained its remoteness and then at the last moment expanded, as if to catch you off guard.

"Holy mojo," he said, bracing himself in his seat like he expected impact. His chains rang like bells.

"It's one of the biggest castles in England. They used to run tours through it, when we were growing up."

"What a magical place to grow up." He narrowed his eyes at me.

"What?"

"I'm just trying to work out how someone who grew up in a castle could stop believing in fairy tales."

"I never believed in fairy tales. Except the one." I circled the fountain, willing the motor to be quiet. I scanned the castle doors, but they stayed shut. For once, it seemed like I might be lucky.

"What are you looking for?" Roan asked as we pulled away from the castle, nearing the garage.

"Macklin. This is sort of his car. And he's sort of obsessed with it."

The garage door was open. As I pulled in, I saw Macklin standing in the spot I'd vacated last night. He moved aside, and I parked the car quick as I could. Then I whacked my head twice on the steering wheel.

"Kitty!" Macklin said. "I can't believe you've taken my car without asking. I was about to phone the police." Macklin ran his hands all over his car, like it was an animal he was soothing, checking its temperature and its undercarriage.

I dragged myself out of the car. "It's a car. It's supposed to be driven."

"You haven't got a license."

"You taught me to drive." I tossed him the key. I had terrible aim, so he had to chase it across the floor.

"Kitty, you can't—"

Roan exited the car. He stood up straight, with his jewelry and his weird eyes. Macklin took two rapid steps back.

"Howdy." Roan drummed his fingers along the top of the car.

"Sorry, I . . ." Macklin colored and played with his hair like Snow White Uncensored. "Who are you?"

Roan blinked at me. He wanted me to explain. Fantastic. "He's a . . ." What exactly was he? A lapse in judgment? A huge mistake? "I've brought him here, to see your mum and Holiday. He's sort of a specialist." Macklin flinched. *Specialist* had become a dirty word around the castle.

"Specializing in what, exactly?"

"I talk to dead people," Roan said.

"You speak to, uh, the, um, dead?" Roan nodded. Macklin's lips formed a firm line. "Kitty, I would never expect something like this from you."

"I didn't realize you held me in such high esteem."

His eyes darkened. "What, so you think this is real? You think this gentleman in jewelry is going to speak to Nikki, is that it?"

"It's not for me, Macklin. It's not for you, either. It's for your mum. And Holiday. We might not understand them but—" I stopped. Was that part of the reason I'd brought Roan there? To make up for not understanding Nikki?

"Well," Macklin said. "I don't want any part in it." He opened the driver's-side door and swung in. "And don't come running to me when you make things worse."

"Is that even possible?" I snapped. I turned to Roan. "Sorry about that. We don't exactly get along. Any of us."

"No problem." Roan shouldered his bag. "You've been through a lot. But that's what I'm here to cure."

I bristled at the word: cure. I wasn't sure if I wanted to be cured. If Nikki weren't haunting us, then where would he fit in our lives?

I jumped as Macklin's door snapped open. "Please may someone get the snake out of my car?"

. . .

I took Roan through the old servants' entrance, then up the stairs so we landed in the Great Hall. The Great Hall was like a stately cavern—dark and seeming to go on to fathomless depths, badly lit by flickering gas lamps.

There were legions of family portraits, so numerous that they overlapped in places. Nikki was the only one who'd ever explained them to me, and he changed their stories to suit his mood, so they always appeared to me as a crowd of shape-shifters. Roan gazed up at them, cradling his aquarium as the gaslight licked his pupils.

"Is it up to your standards?"

He cleared his throat. "It'll do." He gazed into the well of darkness. "You know, if this is going to work, you're going to have to go along with it."

"I'll be all right." Tension played along my shoulders.

"If anything I say or do shocks you"—I opened my mouth to interrupt, but he stopped me with a gesture—"don't interfere."

"I can't promise that." I bristled. "I can't just let you do whatever you want."

That smile again, like he knew something I didn't. Then he started down the hall, in a direction I hadn't indicated. "We should get Holiday first. A mother will follow her child anywhere."

My shoulders hardened but I pressed on, passing him by. "I'll show you where she is." I didn't have to let him lead just yet.

. . .

Holiday's hallway was a swamp of inertia. Roan slowed as we approached, determination setting his features. Lillie, the nurse who had replaced Janelle after the dinner fiasco, leapt up from her chair. "I go in every fifteen minutes to check, but she doesn't like me in there with her."

"It's all right, Lillie." I reached for the doorknob, then turned to face Roan. "I need you to promise you won't say or do anything to upset them."

"How'd you put it? *I can't promise you that.*" He simulated my voice so perfectly that gooseflesh rose along my arms. "But I wouldn't worry too much. Usually the dead don't want to upset people."

"Usually?"

He reached around behind me and opened the door.

Holiday was asleep on the bed, contained in the square blue projection of the television screen. She clung to a mangled pillow, a battered doll that once belonged to Nikki, and a sharp blue crystal. An episode of *Come Dine with Me* played over her. It was funny to think her mum was probably watching the same thing upstairs.

Holiday contracted into a ball. "It hasn't been fifteen minutes!" She pounced, jumping up on the bed and throwing the crystal in one swift motion. Roan caught it in his hand.

Holiday's jaw dropped.

"Get out of bed," he said. "We're going to talk to Nikki."

The color in Holiday's face bled out. Her eyes skidded from Roan to me. I stepped out of the shadows. "Come on, let's go."

"What do you mean?" Holiday said. "We can't speak to Nikki."

"He can." I did not add *allegedly* or *so he claims.*

"How?" Good question.

"Get out of bed and you'll see. Come on. Your mum's coming as well."

She searched my face, like I was the thing she needed to believe in. I felt it run through me, this ribbon of something I couldn't catch.

"Don't look at her. Look at me." Roan bent down, so his chains jingled bewitchingly. He stared into her frightened eyes and he said, "We're going to speak to Nikki."

Holiday nodded, eyes brimming with tears. I had to leave the room. I went into the hallway, where Lillie was scratching at her phone. I gazed down the darkening hallway and wished I could take this back, too. I shouldn't have brought Roan. We weren't going to talk to Nikki. It didn't do us any good to pretend. It just hurt.

I followed them to Lady Bramley's room like a ghost. Holiday threaded her fingers through Roan's, trotted along beside him. It was that easy. Her planet had found a sun to orbit, pulled in by the gravity of faith.

I stayed in the hall while they went into Lady Bramley's

room. I had an appointment with a panic attack. I hyperventilated into my hands, which left them dripping wet, so I wiped them again and again on my jeans.

Why was I so affected, if I didn't really believe it? I told myself it was because I was worried it was a bad idea. That it would be my fault again when things went wrong. But what really scared me was that I might slip and fall into belief. That I might believe without planning to or wanting to. Because what would be better actually—to believe Nikki was gone forever or that he was there, on the other side of a mortal accident?

Lady Bramley appeared, pockets overflowing with tissues. I tried to harness my breath, wiped my hands on my jeans and my shirt and my neck.

"What was Nikki's favorite room?" Roan said. "Where do you feel him most?"

"The library," Holiday said. I saw Nikki suddenly, swaying at the top of the iron staircase. "It has to be the library."

I exhaled, tried to push the memory out through my lips, but it stayed there, at the back of my skull, echoing a steady *drip-drip* that prickled my nerves. Roan dropped back to speak to me. "Are you all right?"

"I feel like . . ." I tried to think of the words. "I feel like I'm doing something wrong."

"You are." He smiled. "You're not supposed to talk to the dead."

"Then why do you?"

"I guess I'm not a fan of whoever makes the rules." He moved away from me. "You don't have to come."

There it was, the perfect opportunity to leave. Holiday and Lady Bramley looked back.

"No." I don't know who spoke, but it sounded like my voice. "I want to."

We passed under the archway. The library had once been a chapel and was the oldest part of the castle. An organ crumbled along the wall in rusted veins. The fireplace gaped. In a quiet corner, Nikki's chair had been pushed hard against the wall. Roan walked straight to it and sat down.

• • •

I knew all the hiding places in the castle. Nikki and I cataloged them one summer, so we knew where to go to eavesdrop on anyone. I never thought I would use those places against Nikki, but that afternoon when Lord Bramley took him to see another specialist, I waited in a linen closet beside the master bedroom.

Lady Bramley was watching TV under the covers, where she always retreated when she was worried. Late in the evening, Lord Bramley returned.

"Have you been in here all day?" he asked her.

"I don't know what to do with myself. I wish you would pick up the phone."

"I was driving."

"What did the doctor say?"

"Well, she had a good look at him. Although he wouldn't take that mangy coat off."

"How could she have a good look if he was wearing a coat? Where did he get that thing, anyway?"

"Oh, I don't know. You know how Nikki is. He's always been a bit . . . eccentric. When he gets these ideas into his head, he fixates on them. Remember when he was a little boy and we all had to call him Arthur for six months?"

"This isn't quite the same as calling someone Arthur."

"I didn't say it was. Listen, I've spoken to him in the car and he's promised me things are going to change." Lord Bramley believed that all the ills in the world could be solved by a promise between gentlemen.

"And that's enough?"

"I don't see what else I can do, Olivia. This is the third doctor we've been to see. At a certain point, you have to hope that he'll get it into his thick head to sort himself out."

"Do you think we should bring someone in, to be with him?"

"I don't think it's drugs. All the tests they've run have come up clean." The blankets flapped.

"I don't understand how he can go from being such a good boy to . . . Have you seen? His hair is starting to go white."

"The doctor said that might be a vitamin deficiency. Or else it's genetic. That'd be your side."

"At seventeen?" She paused, and I could almost feel her turning over something, feel the room turn with her. "Aislyn thinks he's possessed."

"Oh God, please don't, Olivia."

"I never would have thought I could believe a thing like that but . . ."

"But what? What shall we do, have an exorcism after supper? It doesn't help Nikki, you saying things like that. Our son has a real problem, Olivia, he doesn't need you corroborating this madness." The bed was upset. "And don't you dare say anything like that to Nikki. The last thing that boy needs is more ideas."

"Where are you going?"

"I think I had better . . . have a moment to myself." That was the night he started sleeping elsewhere. That was the night the castle divided clearly into two camps: on one side was Lady Bramley and Holiday, on the other side was Macklin and Lord Bramley. As usual, I didn't know where I belonged.

EIGHT

A dim light emanated from the stained-glass windows, so the library had a hazy aspect, all of our actions suspended in a cloud. Lady Bramley clung to Holiday's hand, and they were both pale and sickly so they seemed to be part of the same thing.

"Form a circle." Roan shoved Nikki's footrest aside and dragged a round table in front of the chair. The glass lamp fixed to the center shook. He set his doctor's bag on the footrest and removed a candle, a silver lighter, an inkwell pen, and folded parchment paper.

Lady Bramley and Holiday sat at the same time, giving the aura of a ritual. I took a deep breath and sat down beside Roan.

"Does anyone have an item belonging to the deceased?"

"I do." Lady Bramley rifled through her coat, which I noticed was one of Nikki's: gray houndstooth with broad shoulders. She dug through the inside pocket and pulled out a handful of hair, tied off with a ribbon. My heart stung.

Roan's eyes narrowed. "Perfect." He laid it on the table, brushed the strands so they shone. He arranged the other objects with a psychic's feng shui.

My breathing seemed a treacherous thing—rapid, thick, and overflowing. I was practically panting. Perhaps it wasn't real magic, but it was powerful, sitting in Nikki's favorite place with Nikki's favorite people, just thinking about him.

The lighter clicked. The flame wafted in Roan's illuminated hand and lit the candle, which was deep blue. "Who wants to call him?"

My insides quivered with the flame. Lady Bramley rubbed her daughter's shoulder. "Holly, you go ahead, darling."

Roan unfolded the bits of paper, fingers glowing in the candlelight. He set one down in front of Holiday. "Write Nikki's name, seven times." He handed her a pen.

Holiday wrote in red dove's-blood ink, the pen scratching, *Nikodemus Bramley* seven times, in nearly the same practiced script Nikki used to write in.

"Tear it in half seven times, and give it to me."

Holiday lifted the paper up and tore it down the middle. It was easy at first, but it got harder, until the pieces were so tiny that she had to stuff them into her fist. She passed them into Roan's open palm.

Roan pressed them together, brought them to his mouth, where he spoke into his cupped hands, mumbled words I couldn't hear, then placed his hands over the candle. The flame burst with a *pop!* His hand swept away and the flame leapt up. The paper was gone.

I had to admit, he was good. He had the right look—striking but also holy—and a serene levity. His eyes were so strange, especially in the dark, that it was easy to believe they looked out onto other worlds, or came from them.

The pieces of the old chapel trembled in the candlelight. The high arches over our heads, the wooden pews along the walls, the thin, glowing veins of the organ, and the air, thick with the spirit—of God or something less far gone.

Roan sighed: an earthy, tired sound.

"Holly," he said. The skin along my back prickled. I was afraid he was going to channel Nikki. Terrified of how much I feared and wanted it. "I want you to write Nikki a message. Whatever you want to say, write it down."

Holiday wrote, slow at first and then faster and faster. She reached the end of the page and turned it over. I envied her: perched forward, one elbow on the table to anchor her, pen flying. What would I say if this were real? Questions lit in a string along the inside of my mouth: Do you forgive me? Do you love me? One question, really.

Holiday finished writing.

"Seven times."

The paper snarled as it tore. She ripped it to shreds, words in pieces. She passed the scraps to Roan, who held them to his mouth again, spoke into them, and placed them over the candle.

This time the page didn't burn straight away. It simmered—if that were even possible—like the flames were taking time to devour every last word.

Roan shut his lantern eyes. His hand shot out, closed over Lady Bramley's. We connected in a chain: her to Holly, Holly to me and then—damp, quivering, so heavy I could hardly lift it—my hand closed over Roan's.

I went to shut my eyes, panicked, saw black spots in the corners of the library. My heart throbbed. It's not real, I warned myself. It's not real. My body was having a harder time believing that.

Roan hummed, and it took my head longer than my heart to realize it was Nikki's song. But it couldn't be. I was losing my mind, could see my sanity strung out in front of me, like a tightrope I was swaying over.

The flame went out. I shut my eyes.

Silence dropped into the center of the circle. I felt the pull, like it was taking us down with it.

"He's here."

Roan spoke fast, into his chest, like he was a conduit for an electrical current, and the electrical current was Nikki. "He's showing me something, a picture—has somebody got a special picture?" I deflated in an instant. "I'm seeing flowers. He says, *Thank you for the flowers.*" It was almost like Roan was trying to be bad. "He says he can't believe you're here—"

A strangled sound emanated, from the other side of the

circle, from the other side of the world. Lady Bramley began to cry, not safely crying, but sobbing. I regretted bringing Roan, believing he could help, believing anything when I should have known better. It was my fault, and all I wanted was to go back, to go back and take this and every last thing back.

Roan hissed beside me, like he'd been burned. His hand grew hot in mine. And then a voice—so pleadingly familiar that tears formed on cue. *"Please, don't cry, Mum. It's not nice to see you crying all the time."*

I felt my body lift, the way I felt sometimes walking into a church, even though I swore up and down I didn't believe in God.

"You know I would have stayed forever if I could. And I am with you, always, even if I do get rather bored watching repeats of Come Dine with Me.*"*

Lady Bramley made a sound like a wave breaking.

"And you as well, Holly. I know it's rather rude, making demands on people when you're dead, but I do wish you wouldn't go off in your separate corners, and Dad and Macklin, either. I wish you would remember more of the nice things about me.

"I don't mean to complain, but it has been rather hard dying in the first place, without having to watch everyone fall apart over it. I know Macklin would say I'm making it all about me. By the way, can you tell him—and don't say this came from me— but can you tell him to slow down in that car of his? You can't stay late, but you can always come early, if you catch my drift."

Roan was good.

His voice was so Nikki that it traveled through me, flicking on switches to lights that had gone out. It was not Nikki through a filter, or *like* Nikki. It was so much Nikki that it bled and bred inside me, made me feel deranged, almost monstrous.

Roan-as-Nikki chatted away, but underneath there was a running news banner in my mind, trying to contextualize as fast as it could: *Of course we would go off in separate corners, that's obvious! And Roan's seen the way Macklin drives his car!*

Roan's grip tightened. I tried to center myself, when the only center I had was a being that didn't exist, wavering like a candle, an electric current, an imitation game through the boy beside me.

I was going to be sick.

"Is there anything you'd like to say to me?"

I felt the question point at me. It was mad, but I recognized the way Nikki's voice curved when it turned in my direction. But it couldn't be. It wasn't real. It wasn't anything but a very dangerous trick.

Lady Bramley asked a few questions, if Nikki was being looked after and if he was okay with the songs they played at his funeral. I tried to concentrate, but my head was unsteady. I needed to get out of that room, away from everyone. I needed to be contained. I was contaminated.

"Was it my fault?"

I broke a sweat. I gulped down the acid that hemmed my throat. Roan's grip tightened, so I went numb up to my elbow.

"No, Mum, of course it's not your fault. And I hope you'll be good enough to impress that fact on everyone. It's like I said: you can always come early, but you can't stay late. And there's nothing that anyone *could have done to prevent it."*

I exhaled, unsure if I was relieved or disappointed because I knew it wasn't real then. Because the real Nikki would know that wasn't true. The real Nikki would know it was my fault.

Holiday took her turn, chatting about Nikki's football team, which had come onto a winner shortly after he died. Roan-as-Nikki made her promise to take Lord Bramley to one of the matches. *"I'm doing all I can for them on my end."*

I was counting time, waiting for it to finish, when Roan-as-Nikki said, *"Kitty?"*

The sound of my name in Nikki's voice so seized me that I had to press my lips tight together to keep from begging him to say it again.

"Yes, Kitty, don't you have a question?" Holiday said.

I didn't have a question for a fake Nikki, and the questions I had for a real one were best kept to myself, but a thought darted through me and was out of my mouth before I could stop it. "What happened when you went back to the canal?"

The air thinned, like whatever spirit Roan had harnessed within himself was backing off. The clocks on the wall beat a jagged retreat.

My fingers slipped in Roan's grip, which had suddenly slackened. Everything had slackened, everything was sliding

96

toward the floor, into the void those words conjured. The body beside me inhaled.

"He can't say."

I felt it ending, felt the fake spirit seeping from my bones. Roan-as-Nikki said *I love you* and *good-bye* to the others. They tried to delay him, talking over ridiculous things like the weather and what we would have for supper that night, in his honor. They must have said *I love you* at least a hundred times.

All I wanted was for it to be over, before I broke down or up or whichever way you went when you had nowhere to go. It wasn't real and it wasn't Nikki, but the longer it went on, the less it seemed to matter. It might not be real, but the feelings were.

The air seemed to ease, separate, like a cloud parting. I took a deep breath. I congratulated myself. I'd made it; I'd made it out alive. And then:

"*Kitty.*" My heart dove, then pounded like a funeral march. "*I'm very sorry to disturb you, but I have to. I just have to. I have to say that I love you. So much more than I ever could have before, if you can believe it. I love you so much more.*"

And then Roan shuddered and the warmth left his hands. And I knew Nikki was gone. Even if I never believed he was there in the first place. I believed he was gone.

• • •

We came out of it in pieces, the way you wake from a heavy dream. I kept my eyes closed for as long as I could. They finally opened on Roan, breathing hard and glowing with a golden vitality.

Lady Bramley embraced him. He pursued his breath unmoved.

"I cannot thank you enough. I cannot thank you enough." She clung to Roan, and Holiday clung to her, both in their night-dresses, like Lazarus's shrunken sisters. Lady Bramley ran her fingers up and down Roan's arm like Nikki still glimmered there.

"I cannot thank you enough. I cannot thank you enough."

Roan gazed at me and his lips cocked slowly, arching with his brow, as if to say, *I told you they'd be happy.*

"Yes, cheers," I said, out of breath. "It was very . . . impressive."

"Yes, well, I'd better shoot. Before it gets dark." It wouldn't be dark for ages, though it was already dark where we were.

"Oh no!" Lady Bramley held him. His chains jangled, tangled in her fingers. "You must stay. You must stay here with us." Her fingers slipped between his, gripping his hand to hers, pressing it to her heart. "You can work here. We can hire you on as Holiday's nurse."

"Oh yes, please." Holiday clambered onto the table in front of him.

"But what will Lord Bramley say?" Roan said.

I rolled my eyes, but I had to admit there was something compelling about him, something feline or reptile or David Bowie. Something that seemed more than human being.

"Never mind him. He'll do what we say. And we'll pay well, of course." Lady Bramley lifted her chin.

Roan's lips tugged at both sides of his face. "I guess I could stay." His eyes ran across the heavenly mural over our heads. "For a while."

Holiday hopped to the floor, swaying at the effort, and pulled him to his feet. "Come on! I'll show you the castle! I'll show you everything! Come, come, come!"

"Yes." Lady Bramley stood up. "And then I'll speak to Lord Bramley. Don't worry. You're here. You're staying, no matter what."

I watched them go. The air seemed to shut behind them. I was alone in the room. The gold-leafed mural burned along the ceiling.

I love you. So much more than I ever could have before, if you can believe it. I love you so much more.

• • •

Nikki was passed out on his bed, the coat spread out over his legs like a battle-worn flag. He stirred as I stood over him. "Kitty."

"I came to see you." I was about to cry, all of a sudden, and I wasn't sure why. I wasn't sure if it was because he was sleeping in that stupid coat like a nutter, or because he'd been avoiding me for weeks; he'd been avoiding me since that night after the canal, when he screamed and sweat through all his clothes like a boy possessed.

"What's the matter?" he said.

"The coat. Can't you take it off to sleep? You must be so uncomfortable."

He blinked like it hurt. That I didn't believe him. That I didn't believe he needed it.

His eyes ran from me to it like it was a real debate. "All right," he said, and then he took it off. He wore a collared shirt underneath. I wanted it off. I wanted nothing between us so I could feel like I was holding on to him, like he wasn't disappearing. I reached for the buttons but he put his hand up. "No."

"Nik-ki."

His expression dropped, and I saw how sad he was, how lost. Only I didn't understand where it came from, or else I didn't believe it, which amounted to the same thing.

"I'm sorry," I said, even though I wasn't. "It's fine." Even though it wasn't. And then I crawled onto my side of the bed. He laid the stupid coat over the blanket.

I breathed him in, but he smelled different. I used to love the way Nikki smelled; I thought about it all the time, how people said that's where attraction came from—the scent of your true love. But Nikki smelled different—not bad, but like a different person. It was like someone had stolen something from him, only I didn't know how or what.

"I don't know what that psychic did to you."

He stiffened. "What do you mean?"

"It just seems like . . ." It was hard to say; it sounded silly.

"It seems like ever since that day at the canal, you've been different." I didn't mention that he seemed to be getting worse, his face more haunted, his strides greater—a racing Atlas who propelled the world instead of held it. And these lucid moments, more precious as they narrowed. "It's like you're not the same as you were before."

"I'm not the same."

"But it's— Don't you see? It's only because you believe it. You're under your own spell." I wanted to shake him, to wake him up. "Nikki, whatever it is, whatever it is that you believe happened that day, it isn't real. You're making things happen; you're making things happen because you've tricked yourself. It's like that stupid sign said: it only works if you believe it."

"No. That's not true. I promise you. It works either way."

NINE

The nurse's room had been cleared in a hurry. The sheets were stripped and the drawers left open. The air had a thick lemon scent. Roan's aquarium was on the windowsill, the snake curled in one corner.

Clearly Roan was a liar, the séance proved it. I couldn't trust anything he said. Someone who had worked inside the castle must have given him information about Nikki. I didn't know who—probably one of Holiday's three hundred and sixty-five (give or take) nurses. And now he was using it to take the Bramleys' money.

If he did have tricks, I thought I would find them in his leather doctor's bag. I didn't know exactly what I was looking for, but I needed to find proof. Proof that he was a fraud. Proof that Nikki wasn't really there. It wasn't that I believed Roan had spoken to Nikki—he had been much cleverer than that. He had made me want to believe it.

I rushed into the room and shut the door behind me. I

searched the dresser. A couple of torn white shirts, jeans, and boxer shorts were folded inside. I scanned the floor and searched the closet. I even looked in the en-suite. No bag. I got down on my stomach to check under the bed, when I heard Holiday squeal. She and Roan passed through the hallway, her exclaiming, "I want to show you my essential oils!" The wall shuddered as they moved into Holiday's room.

I was about to back out from under the bed and leave before they came back, when I heard Roan through the walls. "Oh no, no, no." I moved closer to the wall. "You shouldn't have your room like this. You're inviting bad spirits."

"What do you mean?" Holiday said in a small voice.

"I mean, the way all these objects are arranged. And the coat. And the— Is that a blood-stained sword?" I cringed.

"It's *Nikki's* sword."

Roan sighed. I heard the squeak of the springs as he sat on the bed. "Don't you want to attract good spirits?" I wondered if no spirits was an option.

Holiday was quiet for a while, considering. "Is Nikki a good spirit or a bad spirit?"

I held my breath, waiting for his answer. "What do you think?" he finally said, which seemed like a fairly noncommittal answer.

"He didn't seem very good in the end."

"Well, do you ever feel like Nikki is in here with you?" Roan spoke very seriously. It was just the way Holiday would want to be talked to, just the way she *should* be talked to. It made me want to like him. Maybe he was a con artist, but was it possible there was such a thing as a good con?

"No, I suppose not," Holiday said.

"So we change it. Make it more of a haunted hangout." I smiled. Why hadn't I—or any of us—tried to change Holly's bedroom?

"How do we do that?" she said.

The bed squeaked again, and I heard Roan move through the room. "I mean, that's a start. I can show you how to build an altar out of all that stuff on your dresser. And you need to have this coat cleaned. And the sword, too."

"But it's Nikki's blood," Holiday said. "And maybe Nikki is a bad spirit. He's in hell. Because of what he did."

I lost my breath, fast. My ear thudded as I pressed it against the wall. "He's not in hell," Roan said.

"How do you know?" Holiday's voice was strange with hope.

"Because there is no hell. I've seen into the afterlife, remember? There's no hell, but don't tell anyone, or they might start thinking there aren't any rules."

• • •

I slid out from under the bed, opened the bedroom door, and ran smack into Roan.

"I was looking for you," I said, messing with my jacket.

"Looking for me?" he repeated, like he knew exactly what I was looking for.

"And Holly."

"She's taking a nap." He slipped past me into the room. He set his doctor's bag down on the floor. "The afterlife can be draining." He rubbed his eyes, then pulled his shirt over his head and tossed it into an open drawer. His flaming tattoo rippled like real fire.

I shut the door behind me. "You were very good."

His shoulders stiffened. "Are you in love with me now?"

"Not really, mate."

He laughed and hopped onto the bed. His chains rattled. "Well, you wouldn't be the first." His stomach muscles contracted as he propped himself up.

"Funny he didn't want to talk about the canal," I edged.

"It's not surprising."

"Why not?"

"The dead can see the future. Or maybe time doesn't exist for them." He fluttered his hand dismissively. "Either way, they'll never share information that might interfere with something that's, quote-unquote, 'supposed to happen.'"

"Why quote-unquote?"

"The dead are all about fate. It's like a cult up there."

"How convenient," I said. He pulled his bag off the floor and rifled through it. I leaned forward, trying to glimpse inside.

"Now about this other cult. How long do you think it's going to take to track them down?"

"It's better if you don't think in terms of time."

"You better be joking." I was getting a little tired of his philosophical posturing. He pulled rolling papers, a bag of herbs, and the silver lighter from his bag and set them on the dresser. "You can't smoke in here." Was he mad? This was a thousand-year-old castle. Every room was fitted with sprinklers. And while I didn't know exactly what he was smoking, I doubted he bought it over the counter.

"I can see the future, remember? *I'm* not going to start a fire." I rolled my eyes, and he rolled his cigarette, then stuck it between his lips and lit it. "They'll come when you're ready, so get ready."

"And how do I do that?"

He expelled smoke. "Maybe you should try to understand what it is you're looking for. You know where to start."

I moved toward the door, put my hand on the knob as my heartbeat fluttered, tickling me awake. Because I wanted to ask him one last question. I wanted to ask why he'd said *I love you more.* But I couldn't escape the feeling I would be asking the wrong person.

• • •

I kept Mum's things in a box at the back of my closet. They seemed to get smaller every year, even though I never used them. I moved my winter boots out of the way and freed the cardboard box from the closet, dragged it out onto the rug in front of me.

It was filled with mystical things Roan might recognize—the half-burned sage Nikki had used to draw a protection circle, several seven-day Seven African Powers prayer candles, crystals, and saint cards. I took them all out, arranged them in a circle around me.

I reached the bottom of the box and lifted out Mum's book, set it on the floor at the center of the circle. It bulged in a triangular shape, chock-full of pictures and cutouts.

I cracked open the cover.

I didn't know much about the origins of Mum's book, except that she made it when she was young and *trying to figure things out*. On the inside cover she had written in colored Sharpie pens that bled three pages deep, *The Book of Saints*. Every page thereafter identified a saint or a god or a deity from any and every religion, all over the world. So Damballa was followed by Allah and Yama, and St. Joan of Arc shared a page with Santa Muerte. Each page had a picture, drawn or printed or painted, and a list of their specialties, which ranged from mercy, wisdom, and virtue to court cases and drug trafficking.

There was no explanation of what you were supposed to do with the deities, and Mum had never explained to me why she had to collect them all, but I still got gooseflesh as I turned the pages. Even though they were born in cultures and worlds and generations apart, when placed side by side without preference or prejudice, I could see the threads that connected them all. An army of saints.

The picture this book conjured up, the way all the saints ran together, made the Life and Death Parade take shape in my mind—in a train of belief, like a snake, like a ribbon, all connected, all connected to life and death in a way I wasn't. I set my jaw. I had to keep Roan close, even if I couldn't trust him— at least until I knew more about the Life and Death Parade. I sensed they had answers, about more than what had happened that night.

I didn't believe in magic. But what if I could?

My favorite saint was the last one, although I knew it couldn't be serious. It wasn't the last page in the book, but it was the last one Mum had filled—a photograph of herself printed on cheap computer paper. Her name was at the top: Darlene Damice. And underneath were all the powers she gave herself.

grief
creativity
new life

• • •

It was the middle of the afternoon, if the clocks were to be believed. I was wandering. I was hoping to find someone specific.

I passed along the perimeter of the library, the oldest part of the house. I heard tired sobs, like they were running out of the force that powered them. I stuck my head under the arch. All the lights were out. And because the windows in the library were stained, they held the dark.

"Hello?" I stepped deeper into the library. "Hello?"

I saw her there, on Nikki's chair, curled up in a ball.

"Holly, what is it?" I knew immediately, but I told myself I shouldn't guess. She blew her nose on her sleeve. I searched her person—for what? I told myself I didn't know. "What is it, Holly?"

She wiped her cheeks again, her face swollen. "It's Nikki." The answer I expected still hit me hard.

"Nikki. Where's Nikki?"

Holiday pushed herself up on one elbow. "He said they were going to die. He said all of them were going to die."

"All of whom?"

A scream answered. Not from Holiday but from far away, buried somewhere in the castle. I ran.

Not the Great Hall, not the dining room, not the automaton room. I listened for a sound to guide me, but I didn't need one. My feet took me there, straight to the weapons room. The Bramleys had an extensive collection of swords and rifles and bayonets.

Nikki was at the center of the room, surrounded by a crowd, and it was so much like it used to be—him entertaining the tourists—that hope wrenched my stomach. Until I saw the pistol.

The crowd remained in a mesmerized semicircle. The guide was losing color by the minute.

"You're in for a real treat; this is a three-hundred-year-old flintlock pistol." Nikki cocked it to demonstrate. "It's been used to kill people—what a piece of history! Now, on the Bramley tours, we don't just like to show you history; we like to make you a part of it." He aimed the gun coolly at the crowd. "Any volunteers?"

"Nikki."

He spun and the gun pointed at me. "Kitty. You're just in time. Would you like to play Russian roulette?" His face was like a flower closed for the night. "I'll go first." A ripple of astonishment ran through the crowd as he pointed the gun at his temple, eyes on mine, and pulled the trigger—never flinching—again and again and again.

That marked the end of the tourist season at the Bramley Castle, or as Nikki termed it thereafter, "hunting season." The Bramleys paid to keep it out of the papers. There was open talk of putting Nikki somewhere, but everyone knew that once he was gone, he wouldn't be back. And if he didn't seem like Nikki anymore, and every day the resemblance was less and less, there was still something of a physical nature—as his hair whitened and his bones sharpened and he seemed to move on invisible strings rather than by muscle and bone—so even then we kept him, we allowed him, like he was the villain we deserved, because we refused to let him go.

TEN

Lord Bramley agreed to the new nurse—why wouldn't he? It was the twenty-fifth nurse he'd hired that year. It wasn't until supper that he saw his little princess hanging off Roan and Lady Bramley beaming her approval. Roan had put his torn shirt back on, and his chains rang as he helped Holiday into her chair.

Lord Bramley sat at the head of the table. Roan sat in Nikki's chair. I hesitated and took my seat. Sonoma served the supper. The room was quiet; Roan's every jingle sounded like the sharpening of a tiny saw.

"So." Lord Bramley picked up his silverware. "Can someone tell me why we've hired Jim Morrison to look after my daughter?"

I laughed, turning it into a cough inside my fist.

"Can you not see the change?" Lady Bramley scooted in her seat.

"Yes, darling, but I'm somewhat concerned about what it might mean," Lord Bramley said.

Roan pursued his supper with a placid expression. Macklin, who supported his dad on everything, was suspiciously silent.

"Oscar, you promised." Lady Bramley put a hand over his wrist, but he moved away.

"Where are your parents?" he said.

"I'm sixteen."

"That's not what I asked." Lord Bramley's lips thinned. I wondered how much Lady Bramley had told him. How much he would be willing to put up with. "We're paying you rather a large sum."

"It's all relative."

"If it's a large sum to me, I can't imagine how much it is to you."

There was a tightness, just circling Roan's lips. "Well, you don't have to pay me and I don't have to stay."

"Glad that's settled."

The lights flickered. Holiday glared at her father, ready to pounce. I had to do something, now, before it was too late. I opened my mouth. I made words come out.

"Don't you think that's sort of irrational?" I said. Wrong words.

"I beg your pardon?" Lord Bramley sat up straight. Macklin dropped his fork. Holiday grinned and moved forward in her seat. I didn't look at Roan.

"I just mean that—it seems like . . ." I drifted off. Lord Bramley cleared his throat, then picked up his knife like that was the end of it, when I suddenly plunged on. "I just mean that no one can ever know, in this life, what happens after, right? I mean, there have been much smarter people than you—I mean, *me.* I mean, all of us."

"I'll drink to that." Macklin lifted his glass.

I shot Macklin a look. "So," I pressed. "You're left with a choice between two options—neither of which can be verified either way as being true, so you can't compare their merits on that basis." Lord Bramley's eye tightened. "You can choose to deny. Or you can choose to believe."

"And I suppose his wages are my tithing?" Lord Bramley tilted his head in Roan's direction.

"Just because his choices benefit him doesn't mean you should make yourself less happy out of spite. Holiday likes him. He's helping her."

"All right, Kitty," Lord Bramley said.

By his tone I knew the conversation was finished, but I couldn't stop myself. "I just think that if you ask him to leave, it would seem like you wanted everyone to be miserable."

"*All right*, Kitty."

Macklin's eyes were double-wide, warning me to stop. But what if Lord Bramley did make Roan leave? I sucked my lip so hard my piercing throbbed. "I just think, with Nikki—"

The table shuddered as he bolted up. "Katherine Damice,

that is enough. You've made your point, dear." He spoke calmly, but there was an angry twist to his lips, and I knew we had gotten very close to the breaking point. What I didn't know was why I wanted to get there.

The room went quiet and I said "Sorry" to fill the space. Macklin was shaking his head. I finally caught Roan's eye. A smile stung the corner of his lips. My cheeks burned.

"This reminds me of something a spirit told me once." Roan leaned speculatively over the table. "It was something his father said to him, actually. 'You have a good life. You've been given everything a boy could possibly want. Why are you determined to ruin it?'" Lord Bramley's head shot up. The air around us seemed to fall. "This boy, he said, you know . . ." Roan waved his finger like he was trying to remember. "He said he wished he'd listened to his father. He wished he'd been a better son, for him. But"—he shrugged—"there you go." He went back to his salad.

Macklin gasped. Holly's jaw dropped. Lord Bramley's eyes had filled with tears. I'd never seen Lord Bramley cry before. I didn't know it was an option.

Lady Bramley's chair scraped back. "Oh, darling!" She threw her hands around his neck. He cried into her shoulder, the way Macklin cried, with perfect posture.

Roan must have quoted something Lord Bramley had said to Nikki once. But how had he guessed? It wasn't impossible. He probably suspected Nikki was a tearaway; he'd died at seventeen. Maybe it was something all fathers said to lost sons. But it was still very, very good.

. . .

I ran into Macklin going up the stairs. He had a bewitched look on his face. It was a symptom of Roan.

"That was something, wasn't it?" I said.

Macklin tugged at his cravat. "Yes, well, I don't really know quite what to think about all that. You certainly stuck your neck out."

"He was going to make him leave."

"Why do you want him to stay?"

I considered telling him everything, about the psychic and Mum and the LDP, but we had already gone too far. There were too many holes I would have to fill in first, to put the story together, to make it all make sense. I wasn't even 100 percent sure I understood it. So all I said was, "I don't know. I like him. I think."

Macklin toyed with his collar. "There are certain people, you know, that have charisma. It makes you like them even if you don't want to. It's chemical."

I smirked. "Why, do you like him?"

"No." The horrible thing about being so pale was that you painted yourself with embarrassment. "That's not what I'm . . . He's a grifter. He's a charlatan. It's his job to make people like him. It's not real."

I sighed. "What is real?" Roan would say it was my choice. Mum would say it was someone else's. "Anyway, you all right?"

He frowned. "I beg your pardon?"

I never asked Macklin how he was. Never. My chest hurt, like my heart was opening in a way I wasn't comfortable with. "I said, um, *you all right?*"

He winced like I was taking shots at him. "Of course I'm—"

"I mean, with everything. With Nikki."

He backed away from me. "What do you . . . I don't . . ." He tripped on a step. "I have to go to bed. I'm going out early tomorrow."

"All right." He shook his head, like I'd done it again, and then hurried up the stairs.

• • •

Roan stayed. He watched *Only Fools and Horses* with Lord Bramley. He taught Holiday card tricks. He divulged all the secrets of the Magic Circle to Lady Bramley. I pressed him about the whereabouts of the LDP and he continued to plead my patience, but he also taught me about them, so even though they might have been miles away, I sometimes fancied I could feel them getting closer. At first Macklin avoided him, but as time passed he would look in occasionally, observing the strange things Roan was teaching Holiday and me.

That afternoon it was how to build an altar. He had cleansed Holiday's room, which involved cleaning and blessing all the objects in it, then smoking it with sage. The coat had been taken in by a very understanding dry-cleaner and came back fresher than it was when Nikki wore it. The sword had bathed for seven days in restorative oils and was now mounted to the wall above her door. Macklin leaned against the door frame. Holiday and I were piled on the bed, and Roan was instructing the class.

"Everyone's practice is slightly different," he said. He had cleared off Holiday's dresser, moved it so it was bathed in the waning sunlight. His doctor's bag was on the floor beside it. He would pull strange things from it, Poppins-like, at odd occasions. I once had a nightmare that I opened it and found nothing inside. "There's no right or wrong way to build an altar. What we're doing today is an ancestral altar, which helps connect you with people who've passed on." I looked to Macklin, expecting him to make a derisive remark, but his face was quite serious. Nikki's picture sat amidst the items on the dresser. He was the only one in the room smiling. "It's the same basic setup as a standard altar, except with a standard altar you're petitioning a saint.

"So you start with a flat surface." He hit the dresser. "Cover it with a white cloth." He lifted an ancient Bramley family tablecloth in antique lace and spread it over the dresser. "Then your pictures." He set the picture of Nikki at the center. An anxious feeling curled in my stomach. I sat up on the bed.

There was something unsettling about Roan's magic, even if it wasn't real. Every night I tossed and turned thinking about what he'd said at the séance: *I love you more*. And I wanted to believe. Sometimes I could feel myself feathering over faith, wanting to test his magic. And it scared me. "Little reminders and things like that. Powerful objects." He scattered the stones Nikki picked up in Cornwall, earth from Nikki's grave. "Your candles at the back." He lit three white candles. White, for contacting the dead. "Your incense." The smell of frankincense bled through the room. "Your bowl of water." He touched the crystal glass. "Your food bowl."

"Are you going to feed him?" Macklin made a face.

Roan turned toward him. "Well, some people, they actually put a portion of a meal in every day."

"And it just sits there?"

"Until the next day." Roan flicked his hair back. "Personally, I prefer fennel seeds."

"Fennel seeds?'

"Yeah, you put them in a bag and attach them to the back of the picture." Roan produced a little bag. Macklin made a quizzical face. "To feed the spirit," Roan explained.

Macklin blew his hair. "Where on earth did you pick this up?"

"My boyfriend taught me, mostly. Everyone has a slightly different way of accessing the spirit world, so you do whatever works for you."

"Boyfriend?" Macklin repeated.

"Late boyfriend," Roan said back.

Macklin hunched his shoulders. "And you actually believe this rubbish works?"

"I like the ritual of it. I mean, the point of all this is to access something that's already inside you." He made a fist over his heart. "Our minds were created to function in this world. Anything outside of it—the afterlife—appears to us as madness. Sometimes it helps to give that madness a structure. That's why people build religions, to contain something that can't be contained. To explain something that can't be explained. To take aim against chaos." He winked and clucked his tongue, which was sort of his signature move.

"To feed a photograph."

"You're getting bogged down in the details. It's what's underneath that counts. You know Nikki has been trying to contact you, and this is exactly why he can't."

I jumped up as Macklin shoved himself off the doorway. "Don't talk to me about Nikki," he snapped. "You don't know anything about him." Macklin turned on his heel and left. Roan moved back to the altar like he wasn't bothered.

"You shouldn't say things like that," I sighed, after Macklin's footsteps had receded.

Roan frowned. "He just comes here and makes fun of everything."

"It's actually quite a big deal that he comes at all." His bag was lying open on the floor. I slid toward the end of the bed. "I think you should go talk to him. Make sure he's all right."

"Me?"

"You're the only one he'll listen to."

He gave me a quizzical look. "He just ran away from me."

"Because he wants you to follow him." I bounced my foot against the side of the dresser, trying to look casual.

Roan looked me up and down, then cocked his head. "No problem."

He was gone not five minutes when I said to Holiday, "Maybe you should make sure Roan's all right." She leapt right off the bed, happy to be included.

Then the pounding started in my ears. I slid to the edge of the bed. The door was open and I jumped up to close it, tripping as I rushed across the room. I turned the lock, then got down on the floor. My heart raced. I remembered the dream, the empty bag, the real magic, and then I pulled the bag toward me, pulled apart the stiff wooden mouth. I reached into it and quickly retracted my hand: the feathery tickle of human hair.

I took a deep breath, double-checked the door, and turned the bag over.

Crystals and candles and liquid vials spewed across the floor in a cough of dirt. Roan may have kept his boat neat, but his bag was disgusting. There was a rusted folding knife with inlaid gold horses, a broken harmonica held together by a bobby pin, and locks of human hair, tied off with ribbons, that came apart in my hands and stuck in strands to my jeans. Last to fall was a book handmade from recycled paper. It had no title but inside it were diagrams and lists: *fast for seven days, bathe in blessed oils.* Items listed alongside their intentions. *Pigeon manure: jinxing. Snake sheds: revenge.* One diagram showed a body splayed on the floor, tied to five points of a star. I shivered.

I sifted through the items in the bag, trying to find something that might tell me where to find the LDP, whether I could trust Roan to take me to them, but all I found was more magic junk. I sighed and put things back, piece by piece, cringing as I returned the human hair. My fingers closed around a spool of black ribbon, marked down to half price. I knew what that meant. I had two strands tied around the lucky rabbit's foot: one for the rabbit and one for Nikki.

I picked up the last item: a woven bag. I held it up for a moment, fingers rubbing the satiny fabric. Then I pulled apart the strings. It was grimy and stank of vanilla. I held it up to the light. There were dead flower petals—white with rusted pink around the edges. There were stones of rose quartz and aquamarine. Dried leaves. A gold ring that looked almost familiar.

I stuck my fingers into the bag, felt human hair. This time I didn't flinch. I pulled it from the bag. The light of the candles waved over it. It fell from my fingers and landed on the floor.

It wasn't. Surely a million boys had hair that color, that

golden blond with strands of near-white. But somehow I knew. Somehow I was sure that at the center of a bag filled with magical objects was a lock of Nikki's hair.

• • •

The box was torn open. The crystals cracked. The wax candles flattened, bitten in places. The sage, burned to ashes, drawn along the floor to spell the word: die. *All of Mum's things were scattered across the floor, like an animal had torn through them, like a demon possessed.*

I found Nikki on his chair, his lips pursed, eyes like a clock ticking down. The white hair was prominent now, in great tufts above his ears.

He was alone. He had his sword, and he was running it back and forth along his chest, over the thick canvas of his coat, and muttering, sometimes humming, to himself in that great, quiet chapel.

"What are you doing?"

He ran the sword once, slowly over his own heart, then rested the tip on the floor. "Thinking."

"About what?"

He looked up at the ceiling. "Destiny." He put one foot on the floor. "I used to think only the good things were meant to happen, but that's stupid, isn't it? Of course bad things are meant to happen, too." He stood up, dragging the sword along the floor behind him and looking up at the ceiling.

"Why did you do it?"

"What?"

"The gun. The tourists. I don't understand."

He cringed. "They can't be here. It's not safe. For any of you."

"Why not?"

"Because of me. Because I'm here."

"What's so bad about you?"

The sword scraped in an arc as he turned to face me. "If I told you, you'd make me leave."

"No. I wouldn't. Nikki, you know I wouldn't. I'd stand by you whatever happened." But even as I spoke I was scared. Had he done something? Had he hurt someone? And could I stand by him really, if he had? I saw the pale faces of the crowd. Heard the click of the gun. Saw the silver stabbed into the soft flesh of his temple.

He took my hand. "There's one thing you can do for me."

"What? I'll do anything."

His breath was hot along my ear, his lips shifted in my hair. "Pray for me. As hard as you can. Pray for me." He gripped my wrist and the sword clattered to the floor, and my knees swayed.

I did pray that night, even though it seemed stupid and surreal. I prayed over and over: Please, God, help Nikki.

And I felt sure things would be all right. I believed he would be saved. I had no idea how far he'd already gone.

ELEVEN

I waited ages for Roan to return, clutching the hair in my fist. I held it to my nose. I recognized the patchouli scent of Nikki's shampoo. Roan didn't come back. So I went looking for him, tucking the woven bag in the pocket of my army coat.

I found him in the aviary with Holiday. He had a bird on his wrist, pecking seeds from his open palm. Holiday watched, mystified. He looked up when he saw me, but he moved so smoothly that the bird didn't flinch.

"I need to speak to you," I said. "Alone."

Holiday bounced forward, sensing he was in trouble. "Macklin tried to kiss him, but then Macklin ran away again."

My jaw dropped. Gooseflesh ran up and down my shoulders. "Now."

The bird fluttered its wings manically but stayed on his wrist until he flicked it off. "Sure." He ruffled Holiday's hair. "I'll be right back."

"Can't I come?" she said.

He bent down and passed the seeds to her. "When I get back I want to see them eating from your hand." He held a finger up between her eyes. "Remember, you have to stay perfectly still. Don't even breathe." She nodded, half-gasping, and stretched her arm up high.

I led Roan through the glass doors, out of the aviary, and into the automaton room. He strode around the room, observing the glass-eyed miniature faces with disdain. He swiveled to face me. "Has anyone ever told you that you live in a horror movie?"

"Are you auditioning for the villain?"

"What did I do? All I've done is help you, all of you."

"Did Macklin really try to kiss you?"

"I can't control other people."

"No? Then what's this for?" I pulled the bag from my pocket.

His eyes widened and contracted, like lenses adjusting, focusing on me. It was the first time I had ever seen him taken by surprise. "And I'm the villain? What about my right to privacy?"

"What is it? Some sort of curse?" Nikki had said he was cursed; what if he was right?

"What if it was? You wouldn't believe it anyway." He reached for it, but I held it out away from him.

"You knew Nikki," I said.

"I met him at a party."

I shook the bag. "Why have you made this?"

"He asked me to." He sat down in a chair, tossed his hair out of his eyes. "I made it for him. I was going to give it to you."

"Why?"

"It's a love spell." He drew his finger along the antique armrest. "I assumed it was for you."

"Oh, really?"

He took the bag from me and pulled the items out one by one. "Rose quartz and aquamarine and spearmint leaves. A wedding ring." He set them on a side table. "If you'd ever listened to your mother, you would know all of this. It means *love*. Google it."

"Why didn't you tell me you'd met him?"

"Because of this." He blew air from his lips. "Because of exactly what's happening now. I was waiting for you to trust me." He stood smoothly so he was inches from me. "I figured I'd have a long wait."

"You're a liar."

"You brought me here to lie." He ran his fingers along a table, until they closed around a turquoise jewelry box. He picked it up and wound the golden key, slowly, so it cranked beneath our words.

"Why have you kept it?"

"He lost it." The cranking grew louder as it tightened. His knuckles whitened. "You know how he was always losing things."

"*That's* how you knew. You spoke to him at the party. That's how you faked all of this, the reading, the séance. I *do* know what Nikki was like. He'd tell a stranger everything. He told you, everything." Roan said nothing. Even still he wouldn't admit it. "You're a fraud."

"You brought me here to be a fraud."

"I know." I stepped forward, but my voice betrayed me. My breath stuck inside my throat. Of course I knew he was a liar, of course I knew he was a fraud. But it was one thing knowing and another thing believing. And maybe I had believed, for one small moment in one small way, that the things he said could be real. "I don't want you here anymore."

"I thought I wasn't here for you." The music box crackled as he made one final crank. "I thought I was here for them." He swung his hair toward Holiday, who I could see through the door, beyond the glass, was balancing a bird on her fingers. He set the jewelry box on the table; the mechanical bird rollicked into a dizzy, jerking spin. The music played too fast, the mechanism wound too tight. "Seems like I'm not the only liar around here."

"That's it. You're leaving."

"Then I guess this is good-bye." He clucked his tongue as he winked and left the room.

I watched him reappear beyond the glass. Holiday squealed with delight. The bird shot back into the air. Beside me, the mechanical bird swung and rattled.

Roan knew Nikki. What else was he hiding? I didn't believe

him anymore. I didn't believe he didn't know exactly what he was doing, with Macklin, with everyone. I had to get him out of the castle, before he cast a spell I couldn't uncast. I started down the hall toward Lord Bramley's office but found Macklin loitering in the hallway, watching Roan inside the aviary.

"What are you doing here?"

Macklin fussed with his collar. "I was just bored." He gazed back toward the pair. "You have to admit, he's not boring."

"I'm getting rid of him. You'll have to find other ways to entertain yourself."

Macklin yanked his collar so hard it nearly tore. "But you brought him here." His brow furrowed. "You defended him. All that rubbish at the table."

"He's not who I thought he was. He knew Nikki. They met before. That's how he knows all about him. And he's used it to trick us."

"Isn't that what you asked him to do?" Not this again.

"Whose side are you on?"

Macklin took his car keys out of his pocket and wound them around his finger. "What about this group, this life and death group?"

"How do you know about that?"

"I'm not a complete ninny, you know. I do notice things. He's mentioned them, with Holiday."

"It's this sort of cult, I guess. My mum used to belong to it." I slipped Nikki's rabbit's foot out of my pocket without thinking, untangling the knots in the ribbon. "He's supposed to take me to them. Although knowing him, that's probably a lie as well."

"It's the party Nikki went to, isn't it? The one he talked about that day, with the snakes. The funeral." Macklin inhaled slowly. "That must be where Roan met Nikki." Everything was moving closer and closer together. "That's where you'll find your answers, isn't it?" He took the rabbit's foot from my hand and pulled loose the knots for me, set them straight, and handed it back. "If you make him leave, we'll never find them."

"But I can't even trust him to tell me."

"Maybe I can help."

"How?"

His expression flickered. "I don't know. I can get close to him. Play good cop to your bad cop. I think. I mean, don't you think he likes me?" The question burned along the inside of my lips, and there it was, the perfect moment to ask him, *Did you really try to kiss him?* But it felt too real. Too intimate. And we didn't speak about things like that, Macklin and I. We hardly spoke at all.

I gazed again beyond the glass; Holiday had caught another bird, and six or seven were strung along Roan's arm. As I watched the birds fidget, hop from foot to foot, Roan's eyes found Macklin's beyond the window and he smiled slightly, like he could hear us through the glass. Macklin waved and smiled back.

● ● ●

Macklin was with Roan all the time. I knew he was supposed to be helping me, but I felt like he'd been waiting for any excuse to get closer to Roan. I hung around, too, kept pressing Roan on the LDP, but I felt pushed out, separated by something.

On sunny afternoons they would gather outside under Nikki's favorite tree. If it rained, they would huddle in the library, read Nikki's favorite books, or paint at his easel. Even Lord and Lady Bramley treated Roan sometimes, I thought, with too much affection, teasing him about his jewelry, calling out to him when a Rolling Stones documentary was on so they could all watch it together. And Macklin was either deep under cover or just deep under Roan's spell, because every day he moved closer to him. He hung on Roan's every word, reacted to his every movement, like an instrument tuning itself in his key.

I started carting Mum's book around with me, studying the saints, thinking about what I'd ask for, if I had the faith to ask for anything. I was perusing it one wet afternoon in the library when Roan caught my eye.

He was sitting in Nikki's chair, with his feet crossed over Nikki's footrest—just the way Nikki sat—like some insidious form of chameleon. Macklin was on a chair just beside him, and Holiday was on her belly on the floor, wearing five or six necklaces in homage to her leader.

"Do you know what would be really nice right now?" Roan said. "A cup of English tea. Macklin, would you get some for me? Holiday can help."

Macklin was the last person I ever expected to see taking orders, but he shut his book and stood up, stretching.

"Macklin." I stiffened. "You don't have to do what he says."

Macklin rubbed the back of his neck. "Don't you want tea?" He helped Holiday to her feet, and they both went off together.

I sat up, itchy under the skin. "I don't understand why everyone does everything you want."

"And why they don't do the same for you?" He turned the page of an illustrated copy of Dante's *Inferno*. "Because you never ask for it. You ask for nothing, so that's what you get." He scanned the drawing, then met my eyes. "You could have everything you want if you would just ask."

I glared at him. "I want to know where this bloody group is."

"They should be here soon." He looked out the window, as if it might be written in the sky. "But that's not what you really want, is it?" He elbowed himself up.

"I want you to leave."

He scoffed. "You don't like me."

"Oh, I absolutely adore you. I just don't trust you."

He sighed, ran his fingers through his lank hair. "Ask. Ask for anything you want."

"All right, then." My lungs expanded on a breath. My voice was stone-cold. "I want Nikki back."

He laughed once. "Maybe we should start a little smaller. You want to find the Life and Death Parade? Find them. When you go upstairs tonight to sleep, build an altar, light a candle, chant—do whatever you need to do to believe, and then ask for it."

"That's not how things work."

"Who cares *how* things work, as long as they work?" China cups jingled as Macklin and Holiday came through the door. "See?" Roan winked. "Everything you want."

• • •

I woke up at three o'clock in the morning, the time Mum said the veil between this world and the next was thinnest. I took a deep breath and swung my feet to the floor.

You start with a flat surface.

My dresser was cluttered with pictures of Nikki, Macklin, and me, stones from the beach, notes he'd written (*Kitty, where are you? I miss you*). I cleared them carefully away, set them on the floor, until the dresser was clean.

Cover it with a white cloth.

I stripped the case from my pillow, spread it over the dresser, pulled the corners so it lay flat.

Then your pictures.

I lifted Mum's book from my bedside table and flipped to the back, until I found her picture. I used an old sketchbook as a straight edge and tore it from the book. I leaned it against the wall, at the center of the dresser. A funny feeling curled in my stomach. There was something unsettling about altars and objects and magic, even if you didn't believe in them.

Powerful objects.

I pulled the rabbit's foot from my pocket, the spell bag from my drawer. I arranged them artfully on the dresser.

Your candles at the back.

I had a candle we got in Paris, with pictures of the Eiffel Tower and the Champs-Elysées. It was meant to smell of lavender. It was cream-colored, not white, but Roan said it was only your intention that mattered. I lit the wick.

I went to the sink and poured a cup of water. I watched the light flicker and pool over the surface. I wasn't sure what to do with my hands, so I clasped them together. Was I supposed to shut my eyes? Should I get down on my knees? I didn't know. All I knew was that I was supposed to ask, so I did it out loud, over and over.

"Let me find the Life and Death Parade. Let me find the Life and Death Parade. . . . Please, Mum."

I asked for ages, until my mind spun and I started to feel faint. Then I left the altar and crawled back into bed, watched the candlelight flicker on the ceiling until I fell asleep.

• • •

I awoke to a sharp tweeting sound. The stench of smoke, thick in my throat. I sat up in bed. I saw a towering inferno.

I threw my blankets aside. I had lit my room on fire.

I leapt out of bed and stood before the fire, bewitched. Mum's picture was gone; the rabbit's foot was a blackened stump. The spell bag was cooking nicely. I stumbled back, pulled my blanket off the bed, and threw it over. The flames shot toward the ceiling.

A stream of water hit me square in the back. I raced from my room as water pelted down. I had set off the sprinklers, not just in my room, but all down the hall. I ran into Macklin and Lord Bramley.

"What happened?" Macklin said.

"Fire. In my bedroom. It was a candle." They both hurried past me. I stood there dumbly, on the edge of the sprinkler line, watching the water puddle on the old wood.

Once the fire was contained, Lord Bramley asked to speak to me alone. We went into one of the study rooms near the front of the house. Fires were pretty serious in old places like this. And so was water damage. I sat down in a chair across from him as he ran his fingers along his scalp.

"What were you thinking? What were you doing?"

"I wasn't thinking anything. I just left a candle burning. I thought candles put themselves out when they finished." I wanted to explain to him how I hadn't even wanted to burn it in the first place, how Roan told me— Roan, this was all his fault. I sat up straight in my chair. "I'm really sorry, sir. It won't happen again." I gripped the armrests, preparing to get up, to escape while I could. I started to stand.

"That's not the only thing, Kitty." He motioned me down. I collapsed back into the chair. "We've had an email from your school." Drat, email. I could never keep track of what century I was living in. "About your GCSEs."

"I thought the results weren't in until August?" I said, not that it mattered now.

"I'm afraid they're quite easy to predict when you leave your exams blank."

"That's not fair. I didn't leave them *all* blank. I did write something." I prayed they hadn't sent him what I wrote. It was all sort of a blur now, but I didn't recall it being particularly optimistic.

He leaned forward. "Apparently you were off topic."

"Oh," I said. I didn't know what else to say. I hadn't thought about my exams once since I burned the letter; it was like my own magic spell. It was so disorienting—being confronted with reality. It was like being in a dream.

"Kitty," he said calmly. "I think you must have known this was coming."

Of course I knew, but what did that matter? I knew everything would always go wrong forever. But it didn't make it any less shocking.

"Kitty, I'm concerned. You seem to be . . . drifting."

I didn't say anything—what could I say? Of course I was drifting. What else could I do? Only a cold person could say, *The boy I loved is dead, so let's make lemonade out of corpses!* To do anything else but drift would be to corroborate with the world, to agree to all this madness. To say it was okay that people died. To say something good could come out of it. "You need to decide," he said, "what it is that you want."

I thought my answer so intensely I almost believed he would read my mind: *But what if I can't have what I want?* Because what I wanted was impossible. What I wanted was the world to right itself and start over. I could be generous; I could give the world another chance, if it would just give me Nikki back. "Yes, sir."

His expression scrunched. "You don't have to call me sir."

"All right." I didn't know what to call him. I thought of him as Lord Bramley, but that was probably worse than sir. I got up, slightly stooped.

He sighed again. "I suppose you'd better get back to bed. Will you be all right in your mum's room?" I nodded. My cheeks felt heavy, like I was going to cry.

"Thank you," I said, lest I seem ungrateful for being scolded. I shut the door behind me and wandered down the hallway toward Mum's room.

I passed by my desecrated bedroom on the way. Edgar had already peeled back the rugs and was running fans along the hallway. The dresser was an unholy black mass on the floor— nothing was distinguishable, except the hard lump of wax from that tourist trap candle. I couldn't believe it. I had burned Nikki's rabbit's foot, burned his love spell, burned my mum's picture, the page where she'd written: *grief, creativity, new life.*

What was I thinking? Of course it would go wrong. Everything did. I heard someone take a step behind me, heard the jingle of chains.

"Thanks for the advice," I said, turning around to face Roan. "You're a real help."

His smile was limp with moonlight. "Tomorrow night."

"What?"

"They're coming tomorrow night." He leaned against the wall. "I guess they saw your smoke signals."

"You're joking. That's impossible." I stepped forward, caught him by the arm. "You've known all along. You were just waiting for me . . . I don't know what you were waiting for."

He rolled his eyes and pulled his arm away. "I told you," he said, knocking on the wood as he passed through the door frame. "All you have to do is ask. Oh, and"—he spun to face me—"make sure you bring a lot of money. I mean, *a lot*."

"What for?"

"You know how I make a living off the dead?" His teeth glinted. "Well, the Life and Death Parade make a killing."

* * *

I was in the aviary with all the birds whispering, twittering overhead. Their feathers were all colors and so were the leaves and the lights through the sky when he came through the doors, rattled past the chains that hung at the edge of the cage.

He looked up at the ceiling, traced the birds' trajectory along the frozen sky. His cheeks were flushed and his neck pulsed, and I thought, I did that. I prayed him better.

"Can I join you?" he said.

I nodded. I was sitting on the stone wall surrounding a statue of a shepherd and his flock—marble sheep interspersed with wolves.

He exhaled as he sat beside me.

"Are you feeling better?" I said. He hadn't been casting spells or storming around the castle. He seemed calm, reserved, hopeful even. I didn't like to think that it was down to my asking; it scared me. Made it seem like I held his precious fate, his sanity—and mine—like a bird in the palm of my hand.

He shifted to face me, put his fingers to my temple, pulled the fragment of a leaf from my black hair. "I have a feeling," he said, eyelashes cast down so they glittered pale in the gray light, "that everything is going to turn out all right." He looked up again and his eyes had a strange fathomlessness, an endless quality. Like they belonged to someone else, rimmed round and round with eternity.

I put my hand over his. "It is going to be all right," I said.

He turned his hand and closed his fingers around mine. "I think you can save me."

"Yes, yes. Of course I can. I'll do whatever you want."

"No, not what I want. What you're meant to do."

I winced. "Whatever. Whatever it is, it's going to be all right. I promise you." I brought his hand to my lips and kissed it, the knight in distress and his shining damsel. I promised I would save him. God.

What a liar I turned out to be.

TWELVE

The woods were thick and dark. We didn't have a torch, but Roan seemed to glow like a lightning rod en route to a storm.

"What's the rush?" Macklin said, tugging his sleeves from the claws of a passing branch. He had been in a mood the entire drive. I wasn't sure why he'd come at all.

"We don't want to be late," Roan said. "The crowds aren't too bad before midnight, but after . . ."

I hurried behind Roan, dragging a sleepy Holiday. "How will I know where she is?" I needed to locate Nikki's psychic and find out once and for all what happened that night on the canal.

"You'll find her," he said.

"You're going to help me, right? That's why we're here."

Roan's chains jingled as he turned around to face me. "Kitty, we're going to a party. Why don't you try to have fun?"

I put my hands on my hips. "How am I meant to have fun?"

"Like, *ever*?" He huffed, pulled at the ends of his hair. "Look, I get it. You think Nikki died because of something you did."

My eyes ran from Macklin to Holiday. "I don't—" He caught my response in the air with a clap.

"Of course you do. Everyone feels responsible when someone dies." His eyes flicked over all of us. "But no one is, except God. Let me know if you find him in the crowd. Rumor has it, he loves these things." He clicked his tongue under his annoying American wink.

As we pressed on through the woods, I tried to ease the tightness from my muscles, the clench from my jaw. "I know it's not my fault," I eventually managed.

"You might know it, but you don't believe it," Roan said.

We stopped at the edge of the woods. The sky was a pearly dark, like a painter had blended all the stars into the black. A field dipped below us, vanishing into a valley.

"Some party." Macklin arranged his cravat.

My heart pounded on either side of my head. What if this really was a trick? Roan walked carefully ahead of us, as if afraid of upsetting an invisible scene.

"This isn't another one of those you-have-to-believe-it-to-see-it things?" I called after him.

Roan turned around and beckoned us forward, spread his hands over the valley. "They're waiting."

I moved forward first, gripping Holiday's hand. Macklin grabbed her other hand, so we walked together to the edge of the low hill.

"Oh," Holiday said. "That's where the stars went."

Below us, all of the stars had aligned on the lawn. I blinked in confusion until the vision came together. The stars were people holding candles—some red, some white, some rainbow-colored—spread at distant points across the field.

"This doesn't look like a party," Holly said.

"It looks like a vigil," Macklin said. I shivered. That was exactly what it looked like.

"Let's go," Roan said, leading us down the hill into the candlelight. He was all business, back straight, head held high, like this was actually an event in his honor. People looked up as he passed, the undersides of their faces lit by candles. Many of them seemed to recognize him. More than one shuddered as he passed.

"Oi! Roan!" A candle rocked, and a tall man dressed like a pirate rose up beside us.

"Safi," Roan said. They embraced.

"I never expected to see you here again." Safi's eyes traveled over the rest of us. "Where's your man?"

"Still dead."

"Of course he is." He grinned and clapped his shoulder. "Good arrows running into you, as it happens. I have a little side action going later on tonight, if you want to get involved."

He poked a rollie between his teeth and sparked it with a rusty silver lighter. He winked at me; perhaps it was an LDP thing.

"Let's discuss this farther afield." Roan tilted his head and started off away from us.

I grabbed his elbow. "Wait, where are you going?"

"Just a little business. Strictly charlatan." He put his hands up in innocence. I gave him a look. "I'll be right back."

I sighed but released him. Safi slung an arm around Roan's shoulder and they walked off, heads close in together.

Macklin huffed. "Nice of him to abandon us in a field of pyromaniacs."

"You're in a funny mood," I said. "You know why we're here."

Macklin tossed his hair back and stalked away, weaving clumsily through kneeling candle bearers.

"Easy, mate! I left my legs in Scotland, last thing I need is to lose an arm." A girl in an all-terrain wheelchair grinned mischievously at him. She had a flag tied around the back of her chair that read *All my friends are dead.*

"Sorry, I . . . Sorry," he said, coloring in embarrassment.

"You know," she said. "There's nowhere to rush off to. They come here. Right here." She pointed at the ground. "This is the best spot. I've been coming for years. I'm Joy." She reached out her hand to Macklin. "I was named pre-chair. My parents weren't that horrible."

"Macklin."

I stepped forward. "I'm Kitty, and this is Holiday."

"Oi, and I thought Joy was bad." She kept on grinning, but her grin had a sort of mocking quality that I liked. Macklin seemed to have gotten over himself temporarily, and stood there fidgeting with his collar as the red wore out of his face. "So," Joy said. "What brings you to the Life and Death Parade?"

"Um . . ." It was sort of a long story.

"I mean, who did you lose?"

I scanned the quiet field: the gray-haired couple huddled together over a tall white altar candle, the teenage boys with a rainbow candle like a firework clutched between them, and the people alone—most of them were—watching the horizon like they expected the sun to rise in the middle of the night. "Is that why people come here?" I said.

"Of course. All these people"—her hand swept the field— "have lost someone. They come here to find them."

"I thought it was a party?" I said.

"That's one interpretation. You don't know anything about this, do you?" I shook my head. "It's all centered around midnight—the hour before and the hour after." She checked her watch. "They should be coming over that hill soon. They'll set up camp and then at eleven o'clock on the dot, it starts. Everyone has a different interpretation, but I think the first half is about life."

"And the second half?"

"The second half is . . . harder to explain." I got the feeling

Joy didn't want to explain, because if the first half was about life, the second half had to be about the other one.

A shudder ran through the crowd. Necks craned and eyes strained over quivering candles.

Holiday gripped my hand. "What's happening?"

Joy's smile widened. "They're coming."

The crowd went so silent that I could hear the tremble of the breeze through the grass. But it wasn't the wind, I soon realized, as the sound grew heavy and defined. It was footsteps coming through the fields toward us. A boy appeared at the top of the hill, hoisting a large flag that tilted sideways as he slowed. The fabric whipped and I saw the symbol—the black snake and the white snake. It straightened flush behind him as he dove down the hill.

He darted through the scattered crowd, like a star shooting through the candlelit sky. He pulled up three metres from Joy's wheelchair, arched back, and plunged the flag post into the ground. The heavy flag started to fall, so Macklin and I jumped in to help him, stabbing it deep into the earth. The flag steadied, and the boy wiped his brow and smiled at us before racing off.

"I told you this was the best spot," Joy said.

The flag flickered in time with the sound of approaching drums. The boats appeared first, whisked along the canal with sparklers flashing, blue bottles jangling along their roofs. Next were the horse-drawn carriages, painted bright primary colors.

Then came the snakes, a black one on the left and a white one on the right, made of silky fabric and held up by a chain of over a dozen people. Still others were on foot, dressed in wild colors. They hurried through the crowd, filling in all the empty spaces, and started to set up camp.

Tall, pointed tents and long, luxurious marquees seemed to grow from the ground. They rose up like an enchanted world bazaar, a canvas-and-clapboard film set in the middle of a field. The people who built them were all different ages, dressed in all different styles from all different places. Incense bled from every corner, filling the aisles between the tents with a mystical mist.

"Amazing." I smiled in spite of myself. Even Macklin looked impressed. "There are people from everywhere."

Joy nodded. "The It's a Small World of death."

The common thread was that symbol—the two snakes—only it wasn't always the same. Sometimes the snakes were twisted together, sometimes they were biting each other's tails, sometimes they were lined up straight—one over the other—in a serpent "equals" sign.

"It's nearly eleven," Joy said. "I can show you around, if you want." Holiday bounced up and down. We were suddenly at the bustling center of a town, when moments before it had been a field of whispers and silence. It was the closest thing to magic I had ever seen.

"Really? That would be awesome," I said. I was pretty sure

I had never used the word *awesome* in my life, but there was something awe-inspiring about watching a traveling town materialize right before your eyes. I breathed in deeply, convinced I could smell the stars, even if I couldn't see them.

I scanned the path. "What happened to Roan?"

"Who?" Joy turned and her face went still.

Roan had appeared behind Macklin. His arm slithered over Macklin's shoulder. "You ready for this?" he said. Macklin stiffened. "Hey." Roan extended his hand to Joy. "I'm Roan."

She took a long breath and said, "I know who you are."

"Do they have anything to drink?" Macklin broke in hotly.

"Of course," Roan said. "They have this drink called the Kiss of Death."

"Good. Let's have that." Macklin wriggled out from under Roan's arm and stalked off along the narrow path between the tents.

I raised an eyebrow at Roan. "What's with him? He's been in a mood all day." Roan bit his lip. I excused us and led him up the path to speak privately. "Tell me."

He rubbed his arm. "I may have already given him the kiss of death."

"What? When?"

"Last night, when you were burning the house down."

"You kissed? Then why is he upset?"

Roan blew out his cheeks. "He said he loved me."

"*Loved* you? That's a bit fast."

147

"Exactly. And it's not like I'm going to say it back; I'm never going to love anyone else ever again." There was an innocence to his expression that I'd never seen.

"Did you mention that to him?" Macklin had queued up for something—probably something lethal—but I knew he was also staying in sight because he wanted to be followed.

"I might have." Roan watched him with a wistful expression.

My first urge was to tell him to leave Macklin alone, but maybe I hadn't been entirely fair with Roan. He had kept his promise to bring me to the LDP, and while his methods were slightly unsettling, he had helped everyone in the family. And in spite of myself, I thought I understood how he felt—his hot insistence that nothing should ever change, especially not himself. "You like him, don't you?"

"There is something sweet and wicked about him," he allowed, then he scowled like he was angry at his own betrayal. "But it always has to be less. First love is the purest. I don't want less."

"Can't it just be different?" I said, trying out a phrase I had heard elsewhere.

He blinked, doll-like, at me. "What do you think?"

"I don't know." I shook my head. "But if I'm meant to try to have fun, you could try, too." I checked on Holiday, who was watching a woman blow an angel out of glass. Joy was watching us. "Well. Someone has to keep an eye on him. Do you want me

148

to?" It would interfere with my plans, but I couldn't just leave Macklin in a state.

"No." Roan smiled thinly. "It's all right. I'll make sure he doesn't get into trouble. You have fun." He winked. "Different, right?" He squared his shoulders, then strode toward Macklin.

I moved to rejoin the others. Holiday raced to catch me partway. "We have to go this way!" She pointed down a twisted alley. "Joy says there's a River Styx ride and a Four Horsemen of the Apocalypse ride and another ride I can't remember."

"The Flaming Wheel of Death," Joy supplemented.

"We'll skip that one," I said, although all of them sounded a bit dodgy. "Shall we?"

We started down the path, which was laid with white plastic tiles. "I got them to put these in. The ramps and things too," Joy said. "I used to come out with my carer, but I've met so many people now, I can always get help when I need it."

"Is that how you know Roan?"

"I don't know Roan. I know *of* him. He's pretty notorious here."

"Oh yeah? Why is that?" I took Holiday's hand as the path grew more crowded.

"Well, first of all, he and his boyfriend used to run a pretty . . . *controversial* performance," she explained. "But that's not what makes him notorious. It's pretty much accepted that all of this is for show." She spread her hands over the scene. There were musicians performing on stages pulled from the back of horse-drawn carriages, the heavy elixir of food with strange names—God's Chicken and Curse Reversal Curry. There was a huddle of telescopes promising *Star maps to your future!* Yoga tents where people practiced Ashtanga and kundalini. There was even a Catholic chapel, erected from wood, with pews and an altar and walls painted with stained-glass windows.

"For the tourists," I said. There were dozens of signs advertising psychics and mediums and tarot workers. I peered into every tent we passed, keeping my eyes out for Nikki's psychic, getting glimpses of candlelit altars and dangling herbs. My eyes burned from incense.

"Exactly. But along the fringes, there are people who practice *real* rituals. Allegedly. And allegedly, Roan's the real deal. When he dies, he'll become a saint in the LDP, as crazy as that sounds." She indicated stalls selling saint cards. I recognized names from Mum's book, but they were all done in each artist's unique style.

"How do you become a saint?"

"Faith."

"But Roan doesn't believe in anything. You should hear him talk about God."

"He must believe in something. The LDP believe faith is a power, even if it's faith in the 'wrong' thing. They have saints for everything, from flower arranging to getting away with murder. How do you know him?"

"He works for my family. He performed a séance."

"You're joking." She stopped in her tracks. "What was it like? Did it work?"

We were next to a stall selling stuffed toys. I glanced at Holiday. "Why don't you go see if there's one you fancy?" I said, waiting until she was out of earshot to answer Joy. "I don't know." I ignored the way my stomach dipped. "You come here every year. Haven't you ever seen a séance?"

"Oh, no, they're, like, insanely expensive. *Everything* here costs money. They won't even let you watch a petitioning unless you pay."

"Petitioning?"

"Petitioning a saint. There are all sorts of different practices and beliefs in the LDP, but saints are at the center of everything. There are thousands of them, from every corner of the world. Practitioners have altars where they pray to saints for blessings and curses, or to see the future. People pay to have saints petitioned on their behalf, and it's not cheap."

I scanned the scene around us. Money changed hands at every stall. There were signs posted: *Afterlife Elixir £320.00, Blessed Tea £77.70.* "Are those prices real?" I said.

"Oh, yeah, that's the one thing that's definitely real," Joy said. "My second year I really wanted to save up to ask a saint a question—just one question: three thousand pounds. It would have taken me about forty years to save that much. I figured by then, I'd know my future anyway."

Holiday held up a bear with a crooked frown and *X*s for eyes. "Can I get one of these?"

I walked over to the stall and plucked up a unicorn with cracked crystal eyes. It stank of herbs. "They're not very cute." The stall worker watched us from her perch in the corner with the same crooked frown as the teddy bear.

"They're spirit dolls," Joy said. "You buy one and the woman over there performs a ritual to fill it with the spirit of your lost loved one." I dropped the unicorn.

Luckily Holiday was already on to the next thing. She dragged me toward a queue streaming from an orange-and-cream tent. "I want to get my face painted!" It was only eleven pounds, which seemed wildly reasonable just then.

"You should do it," Joy said. "It changes after midnight; it's pretty cool."

I handed Holiday some money, and she got in the queue. I searched the main thoroughfare for any sign of the psychic. "What are you looking for?" Joy said. I gave her the short version of Nikki and the psychic. She cocked her head. "Wait, this Nikki, was he carrying a cane?"

"Yes." I took her hand in excitement. "Did you meet him? Did you see him?" If coincidences hadn't become so ordinary, I might not have believed her, but I had this sudden understanding that everything was linked. In a place like this, it seemed possible.

"Yeah." Her face shone. "I remember him. I remember he

came here alone—he was surrounded by people, but he came alone. We met right before the midnight show. He bought me a cup of Heaven." A smile spread across her lips, remembering. "It's this drink they do that's made out of vapors. It literally evaporates as you're trying to drink it. It's symbolism, I guess. Very expensive symbolism. When the first one disappeared, he bought me another one, which did the exact same thing. And then he said, *I guess it's true what they say, you can't buy your way into heaven* or something like that. He was funny."

"Yes."

Holiday was listening from her place in the queue. "I wish he were here," she said, gazing down the aisles.

"Maybe he is," Joy said. "Everyone's meant to be. That's why people come here, to get a glimpse."

"A glimpse of what?" I said.

"The afterlife."

"Have you had one?"

"Maybe." She looked down at her hands. "I don't know." The music seemed to quiet. She took a deep breath. "The first time I came alone, it started raining. I should have called my carer, but I'd made such a big thing about going alone; I wanted to prove that I could handle it. Then at midnight, the rain stopped, just stopped like magic, but there were still puddles everywhere. Have you ever tried to get a wheelchair through mud? I got stuck and it was dark and I wasn't used to asking people for help yet and I just started crying. Then I looked down at the puddle I was stuck in and I saw the reflection of a rainbow in the sky. After dark. My mum used to love rainbows. I know it's impossible. And it could have been anything, I guess. But I know what it was to me." I nodded, and for once I didn't try to correct the story, didn't try to adjust it so it made sense. I just let it be. "And then these two people appeared—I'll never forget, one was dressed as a skeleton and the other was dressed as a bumblebee—and they helped me back onto the path. There aren't many places where you get rescued by a skeleton *and* a bumblebee."

Holiday reached the front of the line and went into the tent to have her face painted. Joy and I stayed outside to wait, tucked into a corner away from the growing crowd.

Joy wore a serious expression as she observed the crowd. She finally said, "You don't believe in the afterlife, do you?"

I checked Holiday was safely inside the tent. "I don't know. I just think . . ." I shrugged. "If Nikki were out there, he would let me know. That's the first thing he would do."

Joy nodded slowly but said, "If you didn't have an arm, and someone reached out to shake your hand, what would you do? If you didn't have a body and someone asked you to touch them . . . Maybe what you're asking is impossible."

Across from us, four horses danced around a ring—two white and two black. The crowd was growing, and growing wilder. There were packs of people charging around with their faces painted wild colors, dancing and blowing glow-in-the-dark whistles. The air was shifting. Midnight was approaching.

• • •

I awoke to the stench of his coat. The stiff fabric scratched my cheek. I backed up quick, banging my shoulder against the armoire.

"Nikki." I gasped. "What are you doing?"

He looked skeletal in the dark, corpselike. And it was clear in the light of the moon that he was already dying someplace. The whites of his eyes were blushing pink. His lips were blue.

He folded down in front of me. Something flashed through him, the thump of recognition. "I need your help."

I exhaled, pulse in a rhythm beating beneath. "Of course, Nikki. Of course I'll help you." He took my hand, collected it in his bone fingers. One ran along the inside of my wrist. And then he pressed something—heavy and metallic—into my hand. I gasped. "Nikki, what is this?" It was the flintlock pistol, polished like it had been prepared.

He moved over me, so his overgrown hair tickled my neck. His voice throbbed, rasping, in my ear. "It's a gift."

"Why are you giving this to me? Where did you find it?" I thought Lord Bramley had locked it up, or got rid of it, after the incident with the tourists.

He fell back, smiled slightly. "I thought we could do a test."

"What kind of test?"

"A test of fate." He put his hands over mine, cocked the pistol. "We each take turns. First you. Then me. Then the sky. That way we'll know who's supposed to die." He laughed. "It rhymes. I didn't even know it. Hey, don't be sad." He ran a finger down my cheek. "It won't work unless it's meant to."

I held the gun out—which probably wasn't the most balanced decision—and shot it three times. Nikki leapt up, grinning madly.

The second shot left a hole in my bedroom wall.

"You loaded it that way on purpose," I said.

"No, I didn't." He took my hands, jumped up and down. "No, I didn't, Kitty." I felt the castle stir over us—how was I going to explain this? "Don't you see?" He ran to the hole, traced it with his finger. "This just proves it."

Footsteps raced down the hall. I dropped the gun.

"It's fate!"

THIRTEEN

The place was packed. The music shifted to drum and bass, beats so heavy I felt them like a pulse. We had returned to the spot where we first met, under the flag that was now torn to ribbons, rippling at the center of a large ring. A man walked toward it as torches lit in a circle around him. It was Roan's friend Safi.

The crowd shifted uneasily, like a horse being steadied.

"Welcome," Safi said, spreading his arms in a flourish, "to the Life and Death Parade." He bowed deeply, but his top hat stayed fixed to his head. "You have lived your life, but you have come here tonight to die."

"He's speaking metaphorically, right?" I called to Joy over the roar of the crowd.

"You come here to see beyond life." He stretched his arm in an arc, wriggled his fingers in the air like he was calling us forward. "You come here to see into the afterlife. If you look closely." He raised his hand up over his head. "We can show you. If you believe." He raised his other hand so they met in the middle. "You can see."

All the lights went out. I held Holiday as fireworks went off—the piercing run, the deafening boom—only no lights appeared in the sky. There was only the sound running over and over again in total darkness, as if we had all gone blind.

"Why is it so dark?" Holly tugged at my jacket.

The crowd roared as a fire blossomed at the center of the ring—only the fire was shaped like a person. It was shaped like Safi, with long, sizzling hair and top hat lit with flames. Several people screamed. His teeth glowed electric blue. "Welcome to the afterlife," he said, and then the fire went out.

• • •

The entire camp was painted with an undercoating of black-light paint that now appeared in wild greens and blues and pinks. Neon skulls shone, painted on the faces of the crowd.

"This is scary." Holiday pulled my hand and I gasped. Her tiny face had lit up with a secret skull.

"It's okay. It's not real," I said, but my heart was racing. I waited for proper lights to come on, but the crowd was already dispersing. The drums beat faster, narrowing my heart.

"I think I want to go home," Holiday said. I didn't know what to do. On the one hand, I thought I wanted to go home, too. On the other, I still hadn't found the psychic. If I left now, I might never find her.

I crouched down in front of Holiday. Her skull face blazed. "We just have to stay a little longer. I need to—"

"Roan!" Holiday's fear dropped in an instant as she raced to Roan's side.

Macklin collapsed in front of her. "My God! What have they done to you?" he said, running his fingers over her skull paint. Then he planted his face in her neck and smelled her hair.

"What have they done to *you*?" I looked pointedly at Roan.

"I gave him the Kiss of Death." Roan's eyes were like headlights. Macklin stumbled up and threw his arms around Roan, kissed his neck.

"This is getting slightly out of control," I said.

"I can take Holiday," Roan said. "I know a quiet place by the canal."

"I think she wants to go home." I was struggling to be heard over the crowd. Macklin whispered slobbery nothings in Roan's ear.

Holiday was stitched to Roan's side. "I don't want to leave!" she said. "I love this party!"

I felt uneasy leaving them, but Roan knew his way around and I needed to find the psychic. That was why we were here. I nodded to convince myself. "Okay."

I said good-bye to Joy, who didn't want to miss the party. We exchanged numbers. I gave Holiday a kiss. Then I walked alone into the crowd.

I had already searched the tents, but I realized it was

the boats I needed. I headed toward the edge of the camp, to trace my way around until I reached the canal side. The signs gleamed with black-light paint, and the items for sale had taken a darker bent—*Hexing Cream* and *Curse Custard*, *Spirit Spells* and *Hell's Breath*. They were selling dead flowers by the bundle and personalized headstones and caskets. There were shooting games where punters took aim at what looked like real skeletons with what sounded like real bullets. I shivered when I saw a booth called Russian roulette. The game runner sat at the back, waiting for someone to approach.

It was especially mad along the rim, where little splinter groups had formed. In one, people danced wildly to pounding drums. In another, a crowd gathered and just one person danced at the center, juggling two thick snakes. Some of the tents had already been taken down; others had been trampled by the crowds.

The second half was definitely about death.

• • •

The canal was lit up like an electric serpent. People danced to a live band on a flat raft. I walked along the towpath, peered into windows, praying I would find her boat. One boat had a long queue at the side. As I approached it, my stomach flipped. *Psychic, but only if you BELIEVE it.* The sign was posted in the window, yellowed with age. The line went all the way up the low hill. There was no way I would ever be able to see her. I dragged my feet to the back of the line.

Why had I waited so long to look for her? I should have gone first thing. I waited over ten minutes. The line didn't budge. I needed to come up with a plan, fast. I considered arson—I already had experience—but I wasn't particularly good at creating a scene. I wasn't good at getting anything I wanted.

I eavesdropped on the couple in front of me. They were huddled together, talking about the psychic in awed tones. "I've heard she's never been wrong before."

"A mate of mine went to see her last year," I volunteered, stepping toward them.

"Oh really?" one asked. A large group in front of us turned to listen. "What did she say?" The boy beside me was beaming. The group waited with bated breath.

"She told him he was going to die."

The group shifted uncomfortably. The boy frowned. "Oh. How quaint." He looked at his girlfriend. "Is your mate here?" he asked me.

"No." I shook my head. "She's never been wrong."

"So, he's . . ." He peered around behind me.

"Dead."

He pressed his fingers together. "Well." The large group started talking, fast, among themselves.

"I don't really think . . ." the girl said.

161

"Yes, perhaps we should just . . ." They held tight to each other as they abandoned the line. After a minute, the large group did the same. I worked my way down the line, telling the same story. It wasn't my finest moment, but I considered it consumer protection. After all, I doubted the psychic had a Yelp page.

My final predecessor climbed out of the boat looking seasick. There was already a queue behind me. I took a deep breath, climbed onto the deck, and pushed through the door.

The lights were out except for a swirling lavender crystal ball at the center of the table. The woman was behind the table, her head covered in a purple scarf. There was a heavy compression in the room, so thick that my ears popped when I swallowed. The mess on her boat had grown claws over the past year. Old papers were stacked to the ceiling; thick dirt clung to everything. Even the oils couldn't cover the stench, like rotting food.

The woman swayed. "Put the money on the table and sit down on the chair," she said. "And I will tell you the future."

"I don't want to know the future."

"What do you want to know?"

"I want to know the past."

She slid the scarf from her face. She looked older, frailer, like it had been more than a year since we'd met. Not that I'd fared much better. I pressed my tongue against the back of my piercing.

She narrowed her flinty eyes at me. "Who are you? We've met before." I didn't want to tell her about Nikki, not yet.

"I'm Darlene Damice's daughter," I said. It was a card I'd never played before, and I didn't know whether it would have any effect.

She nodded like this didn't surprise her. "Anaya." She held out her hand and I shook it.

"Anaya?" I repeated. "Mum used to talk about you. She used to say, *Anaya taught me how to pray.*"

"Ah." She flicked the switch on her crystal ball so it stopped spinning. "I like to think I'm very good at praying. I always know what to be grateful for. Will you share a cup of tea?"

The adrenaline that had propelled me through the night emptied, and I felt something like dread flood my veins. "I . . ." Anaya knew Mum; they were friends. So why had she told Nikki he was going to die? "I'm all right. I had a whole pitcher of Heaven earlier," I joked.

"Oh God." She threw her hands up. "That tourist tat." She went to the window, flicked aside the curtains, and peered out. The chaos seemed contained now, behind glass, like a circus in a snow globe. "No. You must have some proper tea. The way your mother made." She paused to shake some pills out of a bottle, which she swallowed dry. "Lock the door."

I did as she told me. "You seem nervous."

"Do I? Ha!" She opened and closed cupboard doors, removing pinches of herbs that she mixed in a teapot. "I wonder what your mother would think of all this." She indicated the scene outside. "Not much! When Darlene was part of the parade, it wasn't like this." She wriggled a finger. "It wasn't a theme park. This is for the tourists, you understand?" She stopped to stare into my eyes, like my opinion mattered. "Sit. Please, sit." I sat on the same chair Nikki sat on. "None of the magic tonight is real, but don't let that convince you it's never real."

My heart thudded. I wondered what she would say about her time with Nikki—was that for the tourists, or was it something else?

"Why have you come after midnight?" Her penciled brows came together. "You should have come before."

"I was told that after midnight was for the afterlife."

"Why do you believe what someone tells you? No. You think for yourself, that's the better way." The kettle screamed and she poured out the water. "Before midnight is for working good, blessed magic. After midnight is for dark, cursed magic. That's what I believe, but don't you trust me either. You make up your own mind." She bustled over with the tray and set down cups for each of us. "This is your mother's recipe. Very strong. She doesn't make anything weak." She raised her eyebrows at me.

I found myself warming to her, in spite of myself. There was something hovering in the air, in talking about Mum with someone who actually knew her. It made me feel connected to her in a way I never did anymore. I stared into the murky cup of tea.

"Drink it," she said. "It will give you faith. You need it."

I slid the teacup closer to me. "I don't believe in magic."

"Of course you do." She scoffed, picked up her teacup, and took a messy gulp. She wiped the edges of her mouth. "What you have is the fear. I know. Your mother was the same. You're afraid to believe in anything, but it is only in discovering what you believe in that you can find your true path."

I took a deep breath and lifted the cup. The thick liquid clotted around my lips as I tipped it back. I coughed. "Yuck. This is Mum's recipe?"

"I didn't say it was good, but the best things are neither good or bad."

"I'm pretty sure this is just bad," I said, but I took another sip. I gazed out the windows, which throbbed slightly with the beats outside. "So this is all tricks for tourists?"

"For the tourists, it is." She leaned forward, like she wanted me to ask her to read me. "Tourists, I cold read. It's very easy to tell the future that way." Her eyebrows swiveled as she spoke. "One of the illusions in life is that people change. They don't change. If we met again ten years from now, we will have the same conversation; you will have the same—or similar— worries. Nothing changes."

"That doesn't seem right."

"You watch. You're young now, but when you're old like me, you'll still be young." She grinned.

"So everything is set." My voice rose, thinking of what she'd told Nikki, how he thought there was no way out. "Everyone and everything—nothing we do matters?"

"I didn't say that. You see, Katherine." I bristled; she knew my name. She leaned forward. "You are you and I am me, and out there all different people are themselves. The change is not in you. The change is between you and the others. We are all one being, and together, we make the world. Now." She set her empty cup on the table and walked toward the back of the boat, where the altar I'd noticed a year ago still swayed, wild with candles. "If you won't tell me why you're here, I'll tell you." She lifted a pile of saint cards from the side table. "I will ask your mother—" She pulled a card from the pile and placed it at the center of the altar. I recognized her face immediately; it was so close to my own.

"Why do you have Mum on a saint card?"

"Because your mother is a saint."

"She can't be." I remembered her page in the book, the powers she'd listed: *grief, creativity, new life.* I'd thought it was for fun.

"She is. I use her card all the time. Not for tourists, but for myself. I ask her for things. Talk to her." The idea of people talking to Mum unsettled me. I knew it wasn't real, but that seemed to matter less and less.

"No." My pulse pounded in my throat. "I don't want you to use Mum's card."

Anaya turned. "But you don't believe in magic?"

"And I don't want to know the future," I said. I didn't want to have my future read, my past read, anything read. I felt it like cold water all through me. I wanted to run, out of the boat, into the party, to be lost in beats that never came together. What if I went looking for the truth and the truth found me? What if the truth was staring right back? "I want to know what happened to Nikki. The boy you read for outside the Hartfords' party last year. What happened to him?"

"Boy? What boy?" Her eyebrows flicked with realization. "Ah, you mean the boy with the funny smile, of course. I knew I recognized you. You came onto this boat with him."

"Yes."

"I'm very sorry for your—"

"What happened, when he came back to get his cane?" I gripped the edge of the seat.

"He came back and got it. I gave it to him."

"That's all?"

"We spoke for a while."

"About what?"

"About his reading." She lit the candles that had gone out, so the altar seemed to float with flames. "He was very puzzled by it, as you can imagine. It's not every day you contact the spirit of your dead loved one only to find that you are going to be joining her."

"Dead loved one? You mean Mum?"

"I told you, I always use your mother's card." She brushed

the card's face with her fingers. "Since she passed. She is my most trusted saint."

I lost my grip on the chair, felt my soul slip beneath the table. "You mean Mum told you Nikki was going to die?"

"She told Nikki." She set the matches down and cracked her knuckles. "Now. We do your reading."

"Why didn't she tell me?"

"How could she? You never speak to her," she said. "Let's begin, I don't have all night."

"No." I stood up and stamped my foot. "Put down Mum's card. I don't want you to use Mum's card." I was acting like a child, but I felt the way a child felt, like the whole world was conspiring against me. Mum had told Nikki he was going to die. Mum was the reason he believed it. My mind reeled back to that day with the rabbit, Nikki cuddled into her chest as she brushed his hair and told him *There are no accidents.*

"Darlene will be very angry with me, but if you insist, I will use the serpent spirit." She took Mum's card down and replaced it with a figure that was half man and half snake, a rainbow spouting from his skull. She placed her hands on either side of the altar and dropped her head so the flame from the candles rose along her silhouette like a crown of fire. She began a chant, which I had heard before but could barely remember. It was like watching a memory unfold.

I pushed the tea away from me on the table. What I had swallowed sat thickly in my stomach. I gazed at the party through the crack in the curtain, although it shrank as her chants filled the room. The boat shifted, as if the earth was rearranging itself beneath us. Then she spoke:

"You came to get the blood out." I inhaled sharply. "Of the coat. You came to get the blood out."

"We got the blood out," I said, but my voice was weak. "We took it to the dry cleaner's."

Anaya's back twitched, as if she ran on faulty electricity. "He's showing me a church—"

"We don't go to church," I said quickly. It felt like a battle. Like it was my job to block every assault, in case one did damage.

"—filled with books. That's where it happens." The library. But how could she see that? Not many people filled a church with books.

"What happened?" I braced for impact.

"That's where he dies."

My teeth set. I felt bugs crawl all over me, up and down my skin. Was this what magic felt like? Like someone telling you a truth you never wanted to hear?

She hissed. It set the bugs on my skin alight and I knew I had to leave.

"The one he loves kills him."

I bolted up, upsetting the tea. It ran across the table, spilled over the edge in a long, thin line—the way his blood ran that night.

She didn't turn. She didn't move from her pulsing position at the altar. I reached the door, turned the knob, found it locked. But I'd locked it. Yes, I was the one who locked it and I turned the lock, raced out the door, and caught myself on the deck railing. The party was there, and instead of running away from it, I ran toward it. I ran into the party until it swallowed me up.

• • •

A body fell down the stairs. Thunk-thunk-thunk-thunk-thunk-thunk. I opened my eyes in the dark, unsure of where I was, waiting for reality to surround me.

The wall beside my arm came first, smelling of age beneath thin wallpaper. Then the roof crossed over me, hemmed with Victorian plaster. Then the quiet.

I sat up. I was in the room next to Nikki's. The place I went to keep watch over him, to listen. Only there was nothing to hear. Often I could hear him mumbling but always I could hear him breathing, gurgling as if he were drowning.

I concentrated. The rustle of my nightgown. The rising of my breath. Nothing else. I threw the covers off my makeshift bed. I got to my feet. Nikki's room was only next door, but it seemed to take ages to get there, crawling along the wall with my heart in my throat.

The door was shut. I had a choice. I could open it and risk waking him. Or I could go back to sleep. I checked the grandfather clock across the hall. It was nearly three in the morning.

Just look, I ordered myself. Open the door quietly and look. I broke out in gooseflesh. I didn't like to see him asleep anymore.

I pressed my fingers to the wood of the door, to keep the age-warped wood from creaking. My fingers settled spiderlike around the brass doorknob. The latch clicked, and I pushed the door open without a sound.

The room felt empty, but it often felt that way lately.

I stepped into his bedroom. As I walked, I noticed things, small things, evidence of Nikki: the inkwells he used to write in black leather journals all the contents of his once-magical heart, the iron tea kettle he'd stolen from downstairs so we could have tea parties in his room, the scarf he'd pulled from the beak of a swan. All these things resembled him more than the body on the bed.

I stood over the bed. There was a swollen mass. I reached out, carefully, and pulled back the covers.

Journals. They slid apart, fell open as I revealed them. Piles of them, laid out like a crumbling-paper boy.

The clocks went then. They were all wound to slightly different times, so it was three o'clock, over and over again.

I rushed from the room, down the hall. The stairs stopped me. The clouds pulsed, beyond the great glass windows. I swayed, waited for some sign, but there wasn't one.

Where had Nikki gone?

I started down the stairs, one foot and then the other. I was headed toward the library, I discovered. Toward the chapel.

As I walked through the hallways, the automaton room and the weapons room, I told myself that one day soon I would wake up from this life and find that every bad thing had been a dream. Only the good things had been real.

The weapons are locked in their cases, I thought as I passed the weapons room. I didn't consider why, until I passed the automaton room and thought: You might need one.

The arches glowed. Before the library was a library, when it was a chapel, it was a circular building with arches all around it. It had been merged with the castle, but the joining was hasty, not quite believable. Seen from above it might have looked like the crown wheel of an enormous clock.

I passed under the arch.

Nikki was there, so familiar it soothed me, then unnerved me. He was on the upper level, in stakeout position, in his military coat. There was a fire in the fireplace, too big and billowing; the room was like an oven.

I moved into the center of the room, but he didn't seem to notice me. His face was fixed, his forehead glistened with sweat, and when he wiped his brow, blood remained.

"Nikki," I said, having no idea what else to say.

His eyes contracted. They had a feral quality. "Oh, Kitty," he said in a strange, gravelly voice.

"What are you doing?"

He crossed the balcony and settled at the top of the stairs, resting his elbows on his knees. The fire danced in his eyes, and in *that moment he looked more alive, more himself than he had in weeks. He gestured me forward. "Come here. You've always been so good to me."*

I took a step without thinking. Because it was Nikki.

He stood up, extended his hand. "I've figured it out. I've solved . . . everything."

I stepped toward him again.

"Come on, Kitty. There's a good girl."

I stopped at the bottom of the stairs, at the bottom of the world. The fire leapt up and as it did, lit the golden hilt of a sword, drenched with blood.

"Nikki, whose blood is that?"

"Destiny's. It's destiny's blood." Light washed over him, revealing what looked like black paint. His coat was bleeding.

"Nikki, what have you done?"

He started to shake, like a dog trying to get dry. "I've figured it out. I've figured out what I'm supposed to do: die!" Curled in the twist of his lips was his strange double smile, like even death could be a joke if applied correctly. His chest spat blood in a pulse. His shirt was soaked in it. "I got you something." He pulled a black ribbon from inside his coat, dripping blood. "So you always remember."

His silhouette took on a hot, imaginary quality, as if drawn from a fever dream. His head dropped, took his body with him, and it rattled down the iron stairs, caught halfway by his coat so the blood ran through the slats in a ribbon.

PART 3

When you're held up in a hard place,
Throw a rock from your deep tomb.

—Alan Wass, "Dress Up"

FOURTEEN

I found Joy in the crowd, and we found a place to dance. The neon colors whirled and popped. The stars stayed over my head. They seemed to multiply. I said to Joy, "Look, the stars are here! Look! They came back!" like they hadn't been there all along. Like it wasn't just me who couldn't see them.

"I think we were supposed to meet each other," I told her. "Of all the people in all the party, you knew Nikki. You knew Nikki, and we were supposed to meet each other."

Joy smiled with blue teeth. I understood why she came here, even though she couldn't afford the readings and the tourist tat and even though it was all fake magic. She came because even though it wasn't always real, that didn't mean it wasn't ever real.

The music stopped at one o'clock. The tents all tilted, dropped gently, and descended as people poured out into the night. A few small groups stayed behind, usually surrounding a musician with a guitar. They built small fires and shared stories

I could tell were magical by the way they huddled close together.

"I have to meet my ride. Do you know where you're going?" Joy said as we moved through the field. "Do you want me to stay with you?"

I shook my head. "I mean, yes I know and no you don't need to." I was transfixed by the stars.

"Are you sure you're all right?" she asked me. "Did you drink anything funny?"

"My mum's tea. It gave me faith." I stopped, looked out toward the canal. The boats were gone, leaving behind a dark black river. "It's strange. Anaya said the worst thing she could have possibly said. She confirmed exactly what I was afraid of, but I still feel better." I took a deep breath and smiled shakily at Joy. "I feel better because she knew. She knew things she couldn't possibly know, so it must be real. Nikki must be out there somewhere. And if he is, then it's not over. I can make things right again."

Joy looked unsure. We said good-bye and I went to find the others. I was passing a small bonfire when a boy jumped up and grabbed me by the elbow. "Wait." He moved in close to me so no one would hear. "Do you want to buy a saint card?"

"I thought the party was over," I said.

He shuffled through his pocket, pulled out a deck of cards. "I saw you earlier." He held up an anime-style card with Mum painted on it, surrounded by white orchids. "Has anyone ever told you that you look like a saint?"

I took it out of his hand and held it up to the light. It was perfect. "I burnt mine. How did you know?"

"I had a feeling." He grinned.

"What other cards do you have?" He handed me a key fob of laminated photos. I flipped through the deck: Papa Legba, St. Christopher, Baron Lacroix. I didn't know what I was looking for, but the artist seemed to. He leaned in close, his voice a light rasp. "I also have contraband, special for after hours."

I stopped flipping. "Show me."

He pulled a wad of cards from his coat pocket and handed them to me. These cards were different—rough and unfinished with an ashy smell. I flicked through, one, two. The third card sent a shiver down my spine. "What is this?" I held the card up to him.

"Ah. I know it's bad mojo to make a card for someone who isn't dead, but I couldn't resist." He took the card and flipped it around his fingers, then handed it back to me and winked. "He's my favorite."

It was Roan's card. He had a Peter Pan stance, the snake twisted at his feet. Behind him was a large anatomical heart burning in flames. His powers were listed.

resurrection

youth

obsession

I held one card in each hand, sensing I should keep them separate. "How much for both?"

He quoted an insane price, but I paid it. The boy went back to the bonfire, and I put one card in each pocket, like the two sides of Alice's mushroom.

I was nearing the woods when Holiday came racing to me. Her painted face was smeared with tears. "Kitty, come quick! Macklin says he's going to die."

* * *

Holiday dragged me toward the canal as I tried to figure out what had happened.

"Macklin was asleep," she gasped through pounding breaths. "Then he woke up. Then he went mad."

"Where's Roan?"

"He went with that guy with the top hat." Safi. He'd said he had work for him. I was curious to know just what that work entailed, but first I had to make sure Macklin was all right.

Holiday led me to a quiet spot beside a bridge. Quiet until I heard Macklin vomiting into the canal. Oh, that kind of dying.

Holiday dropped my hand and hunkered down beside him. She clapped him on the back, saying, "There, there," which didn't seem particularly effective. I gazed back at the deflated party, tempted to track down Roan.

"Perhaps I should find you a glass of water." I started toward the field when Macklin burst into tears. I froze. Seconds ticked by and he kept on crying. Finally I said, "Holly, why don't you go fetch some water?" She raced off up the hill, leaving me with Macklin.

I stepped forward carefully. "Um, Macklin? Are you crying?" I needed a second opinion.

"I just don't understand. How?" He drew a silk handkerchief from his pocket and dabbed his eyes. "*How* has this happened?"

"Well, I think it's because you've had too much to drink."

"Don't be obtuse." Tears sorted, he refolded the handkerchief with an origamist's attention. "You know what I mean."

I remembered Anaya's words, *The one he loves kills him.* If only I had done something, said something. "I gave up on him." The words came unfastened before I could fashion them. And once spoken they hung there like a spell. Macklin's eyes met mine in the water. "He believed he was cursed and I didn't believe him. I didn't help him. So what if I thought it was fake magic? It was real to him." Macklin's temple pulsed with thought, but he stayed quiet.

"Why did I have to fight him?" I said. "Why did I have to change his mind? Why couldn't I just see things his way? I see all of this"—I motioned to the abandoned field—"and I think, is it really that bad?"

Macklin chewed the inside of his cheek. "It's a little weird."

"Maybe, but if it helps a person to believe in something, who am I to try and stop them?"

Macklin sighed. "God, will you look at the state of me?" He

181

organized himself by his reflection in the canal. Once he was back to Default Dandy, he roused himself enough to respond. "It's not your fault, Kitty." He inhaled, like he was powering himself up. "Nikki really lost the plot."

"But why? Why did he lose the plot?"

"He thought he was supposed to die."

I moved closer to him. "What did he say that night, after he spoke to Mum?" Macklin gave me an odd look. "I mean, the psychic. Didn't he say anything about it? He used to tell you everything."

Macklin cocked his head, like he was turning something over in his mind. "He didn't say anything. That's when I knew something had changed." He took a hard breath. "I thought he would go back, to the way he was before. I thought things would go back—sometimes it seemed like they would, didn't it?" I nodded. It was strange to have this conversation with Macklin—to have any conversation. But it was a good strange. "He really loved you, you know," he allowed. "He used to tell me all the time. You were like a god to him."

I was temporarily spellbound. It always unmoored me when I heard that Nikki had told someone else he loved me.

"I'm sorry I haven't been . . ." I tried to think of the words. "Whatever I was supposed to be. I'm sorry I haven't been that."

"I'm sorry, too," he expelled on a breath. "I know I must seem cold to you. It's just that sometimes I think if I allow myself to feel things, I won't be able to stop." He said this to the stars. "Like I might just keep going, on and on, until I'm lost forever."

"Yeah. I know exactly what you mean." I stole a moment then, looking at Macklin. He was so beautiful—and then he transformed before my eyes, singed around the edges as if in flames. His pale skin crisp as wax paper, his eyes erased and his hair—his black, ribbon hair—curling in calligraphy patterns across a coffin's pillow.

I lost my breath, turned away to catch it. I was only seeing death because I was surrounded by it. I was only imagining things because the night had filled my head with magic. It wasn't a prophecy. It wasn't real.

Holiday came down the hill carrying a paper cup. "They didn't have water, but the woman gave me de-hex tea. She told me it's really just the ordinary detox tea you buy in the supermarket." Macklin accepted it gratefully.

"I think I've had enough magic for one evening," I said, getting to my feet. "You wait here. I'll go find Roan."

. . .

Smoke rose in a tower at the edge of the woods. The air was wound too tight. There was a carriage parked in the dark, piled with long wooden boxes. Two filthy white horses grazed nearby. Ahead of me, a circle of people gathered around a fire in a small clearing. They were smoking, passing bottles back and forth, and chanting intensely.

Something in the sound made me stop behind the carriage. I pressed flat against it. I pushed my tongue against the back of my piercing until it ached. Then I peered around the side of the carriage. A box rocked over my head, and I nearly jumped out of my skin. Part of the group had moved to the other end of the carriage, not ten metres away from me. Together they dragged one of the boxes from the bed and hoisted it at shoulder height. It was only then that I saw what it was—not a box, but a coffin.

I ducked down, crawled along the dirt beneath the carriage, and watched them carry the coffin toward the fire. They set it down in front of the flames. A woman bent down and started to work the bolts from the sides. Dizziness spun through my veins. They were opening the coffin.

The woman moved slowly; the scene was souplike, murky. I blinked my eyes hard, and for a moment they refused to open. When I finally forced my eyelids apart, they were lifting a body.

I saw everything in shadow: the heaving of the group, the limpness of the corpse, one arm hanging down so it stretched toward the floor. I didn't understand it, or else I did and was lying to myself, the way—I was beginning to suspect—I often did.

I swallowed my unsteadiness and moved closer. Then I saw him. He was on the other side of the fire. He had a snake on his shoulders—tight and coiled. The chanting ascended in volume. I felt my brain narrowing, and even though I couldn't see these details from a distance, I sensed his constant expression. His eyes of crystal, forever glazed. They set the body down in front of him and then moved back.

The chants flooded my eardrums. He reached into his doctor's bag and pulled out a rusty knife. Coolly, he slicked his hair back from his face, and then with his uncanny calmness, he leaned over the corpse, gathered its shirt collar in his fist, and tore it down the center.

I flinched and shut my eyes again. I told myself it wasn't real, ordered myself to watch. I opened my eyes as the knife darted down, into the chest of the corpse. Blood seeped down the sides.

Roan stretched his jaw, then plunged his hand inside the body and pulled out its thick heart. He held it up over his head as the snake tightened on his shoulders. He lowered the heart, and the snake seemed to rattle; it slid up his arm. Its jaw stretched and detached, opened wide. It swallowed the heart whole. Roan bent down and sewed up the corpse as the swell of the heart traveled through the snake's body.

Roan leaned forward; his necklaces hung like a pendulum above the corpse. He pressed his bloody hand against its forehead. The body lurched. The group flew back. The chants snapped into a collective gasp. The fingers of the corpse tightened into fists. Roan sat back. Inside the snake, the heart compressed, in and out, like a heartbeat.

I felt myself move backward. I whacked my head on the bottom of the carriage. I held myself still until my vision cleared.

Then I took Roan's card from my pocket. I focused on the word: *resurrection*. I ran my thumb over it, again and again.

I looked up. I felt his eyes on me, even though he couldn't have possibly seen me from so far. But I saw him, in wild chants, in the manic pant of crowd-think. He appeared to me like some primordial beast, some ancient, tired, uncaring thing. He appeared to me as God.

FIFTEEN

On the cab ride home, my mind was awash with thoughts, but the one that kept rising above the surface was the vision of Roan at the bonfire. If the only difference between real and fake magic was desire, then I knew exactly what I wanted.

Macklin snuffled on my shoulder. Holiday was curled on my lap, small fist gripping the corner of my jacket. Roan kept glancing back at us in the mirror, and I didn't think it was because he knew what I'd seen. It was because of the picture we created, like a tonic for a lonely heart.

There was warmth as we came through the castle doors that night, all of us together, with Lord and Lady Bramley still up waiting for us. Macklin trying not to lean hard on my shoulder. Holiday stitched between Roan's hand and mine. Lady Bramley beamed. Lord Bramley said nothing about the hour.

Instead he said, "Did you have a nice time?" like he hoped we had.

"Yes," I said.

"Macklin especially." Holiday pealed into giggles that echoed through the castle.

Macklin managed to say, "Bed."

"Give your mum a hug first," Lady Bramley said. He did, face turned away as if that could disguise the stench of eighty-proof vomit.

Lord Bramley reached out and brushed Macklin's hair back. It was the first time I'd seen him touch Macklin—not since Nikki died, but ever. Lord Bramley was never one to initiate contact. Even when Nikki had hugged him, often and with reckless abandon, he would only roll his eyes and pat him on the back. Macklin did a good job not to look startled.

Lady Bramley released him, and Macklin carefully directed himself up the stairs. The others weren't far behind. I moved to follow.

"Kitty, I need to speak to you," Lord Bramley said.

"I just have to—" *Ask Roan to resurrect your son.*

"This will only take a minute." Lord Bramley's face was grim. He waited as they disappeared, Lady Bramley with them, up the stairs.

The castle closed around me then, the world whittling itself around the blackness that burned at the heart of the stone. *You thought things had changed, but no, you're back and things are just as they were before.* While any good thing feels fresh and new, it is a unique trait of bad things that they can always pick up exactly where they left off.

"The discussion we had last night," he said. "I could have handled it better." He pulled his collar. "Naturally, it's been a rather difficult year for everyone. But I'm sure that we can speak to someone and you can re-sit your exams. Olivia and I will take care of it this time. It's not your fault. We should have been paying attention."

"It's all right," I said. "I mean, I don't think it really matters to me, university. I don't think it's what I want to do."

Lord Bramley over a year ago would have argued this out. Lord Bramley, even three months ago, would have tried to convince me otherwise. But the new Lord Bramley cocked his head, like this was charmingly whimsical. "Really? What do you think you'll do, then?"

"I want to live on the canal," I said without thinking.

Even the new Lord Bramley couldn't swallow that. "Oh. Well. That's . . . interesting."

"Well, you know, Mum used to travel and I think . . . I want to see things, you know? I want to know things." Now that I'd confessed it, I realized what a brilliant plan it was. Because I could bring Nikki with me. We would have to convince the Bramleys, but once he'd spent some time with them, once they'd settled to the idea that he was back . . .

If we kept him in the castle, someone might see him, and people would start to talk. But out on the canal—where they were apparently resurrecting people all the time—we could slip in and out of people's sights like dreams, dressed like real pirates.

I was actually beaming, just thinking about it. Lord Bramley smiled back. "You know who would love something like that?" He raised his eyebrows, still too damaged to say his name.

Nikki would love it. And I felt sure, suddenly, that everything had happened for a reason. Everything—all of it—had happened so I could have a second chance, so I could love him enough to keep him, so I could have Nikki back.

I raced down the hall toward Roan's room, brain sparking with brilliant ideas. We could borrow Roan's boat—it was already named for us—and Nikki and I could travel up and down the canals, up and down the countryside. I saw us there, as if in heaven, as if in a dream, with the sun drowning itself in its own reflection, with the sky made hazy by hope, with the canal extending on and on as if rising, forever rising, toward some new, impossible horizon.

● ● ●

Roan wasn't in his room. I waited for him, paced the floor, finding fate in my footsteps. Roan was meant to come to the castle. Fate had brought me to his boat. That was why the boat was called *Love*. That was why the songs were the same. That was why everything was connected—*everything*—to bring me here. So Roan could bring Nikki back.

When he didn't return, I searched the castle. I started with the aviary, birds crossing over my head. I called his name. No answer. I tried Holiday's room. The library. The kitchen and the automaton room. But every room was empty, after-hours dark.

I was passing Macklin's hallway when I heard laughter. Yellow light seeped beneath the door. I heard the soothing cadence of Roan's voice, the jingle of his jewelry. I opened the door. They were on the bed, limbs tangled in a cozy web. Macklin scooted back. Roan didn't move an inch.

"Kitty Cat." His eyes flashed.

"We were just having a chat." Macklin slouched, blooming with self-satisfaction.

"Well, I need to have a chat with you." I pointed at Roan.

"Can't we talk later?" Roan's eyes were double bright. The air was super-charged. It was no wonder Macklin was so worried about controlling his feelings. Just one little nudge and they were everywhere. "It's late."

"It's important," I said.

"So is this."

"We could always do it here." I tilted my head at Macklin, who had found himself in the mirror and didn't notice.

Roan sighed and dragged himself off the bed. "I'll be back."

"Where are you going?" Macklin said. "What are you talking about?"

"Kitty bought an academic acuity candle." He brushed Macklin's hair back and kissed the top of his forehead. "She wants me to help her reverse her GCSE results." I was so used to Roan knowing everything that it didn't surprise me that he knew I'd failed my exams.

I led him down the hall and out a side door. He didn't ask where we were going. He followed me out onto the lawn, down the familiar path to the cemetery.

The Bramleys had their own cemetery. Most of the graves were ancient—even Nikki's grandparents were all still alive, one set living on the Bramleys' island north of Scotland, and the others in Key West, Florida, drinking cocktails.

Nikki's monument exuded a disturbing freshness. The ground appeared unsettled, as if there were something churning beneath the surface. It had seemed nice at the time to pick a large, garish monument Nikki would have liked, but in the dark it loomed so large that I had to sit on the grass away from it, keep my eyes on the earth. Lady Bramley brought fresh roses every Sunday, but it was the end of the week and they had faded.

I picked at the weeds around the perimeter. I caressed them, imagined they were growing from Nikki's body—I took it as a good sign that something still lived there—and then I felt sick and corrupted and ruined.

Roan sat down across from me, leaning against a grave so a cross grew from his head. He shut his eyes like he planned to sleep through this.

"Did you have fun at the party?" I said.

"God, it was terrible. Those things get more and more commercial every year."

"Tell me about it. It's all money, money, money. How much did you take home in the end?" He kept his eyes shut. His breath was even, like he might actually be asleep. "I saw you. At the fire."

He frowned. "I told you, that was strictly charlatan. For the tourists. Safi's mates take a nap in the coffins. We get those hearts at a butcher. Someone as smart as you would never fall for it."

I dug my fingers into the dirt. "Just because it wasn't real then, doesn't mean it's never real."

His eyes snapped open. "Kitty, don't tell me the Life and Death Parade has you converted?"

"I want you to bring Nikki back."

"Whoa." He clutched his heart and laughed in surprise. "That party did a number on you. What happened? I didn't think they sold miracles."

"Will you do it?" I crouched forward.

He had a slick smile over his lips, the haughty look I remembered from when he pulled me out of the canal, like life was a game rigged for his amusement. "No. I don't think so."

"What do you mean? Why not?"

"You were right." He pulled a locket from the threads of his necklaces and clicked it open, brushed his thumb over the picture inside. "What you said before the party."

"What stupid thing did I say?" I didn't really hold my past self in highest esteem.

"About Macklin." His face grew wistful. "About *different*." He fixed me with his electric eyes. "I think we both need that, don't you?" He started to stand.

I clamped his wrist and pulled him back down. "You're meant to do this," I said through gritted teeth. "That's why you're here."

He snaked his hand away, then shook his head and clucked his tongue. "Kitty, don't be silly. You don't believe in fate." The gate squeaked as he left me there, alone on Nikki's grave.

• • •

It was like an evil spell, watching people move on. I sat on Nikki's chair in the library for hours, studying Mum's book as they passed by the open doors. Macklin and Roan were together all the time. Roan's arm was always around him, or else his fingers were in his hair or stroking his temples. He watched every word leave his mouth like Macklin was a doll he'd trained to speak. Holiday spent time with them, but she also spent time with friends—actual, living people she invited into the castle. Some she'd met at the party and some were old friends from school, and they ran around in child packs, feeding the birds or winding the automatons or playing the games we used to play, like the games never ended, we just did. Even Lord and Lady Bramley sometimes spoke without arguing, which was really unnerving. Joy texted me about meeting up, but I made excuses. I wasn't going to be like everyone else. I wasn't going to cave. I wasn't going to change.

The anniversary of Nikki's death was days away. Mum had

taught me the importance of powerful dates. Nikki's anniversary was prime resurrection time. The space Nikki had left behind was filling up, and if I didn't hurry, it would close completely. I scoured Mum's book, studying all the saints, searching for one that might be powerful enough to help me.

I was distracted one night over supper, contemplating my resurrection plans when Lady Bramley announced, "We're having a mass read in Westminster for the anniversary, so we'll all be going to London." Fate, my mind pulsed.

"Can I bring a friend?" Holiday said.

"You can bring one friend," Lady Bramley said.

Holiday beamed. Macklin scraped his chair back. "I'm not going," he said. Roan sat beside him in Nikki's chair, which crept closer and closer to Macklin's every meal.

"No one has to go," Lord Bramley said.

"Does that mean I can bring two friends?" Holiday bounced on her seat.

"We'll see," Lady Bramley said. "Macklin might change his mind."

Macklin crossed his fork and knife over his plate. "I'm definitely not going. I'm not Catholic. Also, I'm gay." He stood up. "Can I clear anyone's plate?"

Later on that same night, it warmed me to see Macklin and his dad watching a program about Jaguars, like both nothing and everything had changed. And it made me wonder, sitting across from them, on the other side of the room but feeling farther, if I wasn't, in refusing to change—not even to "move on," but even to keep moving—doing something wrong.

Mum had once said, *Everything happens for a reason, but the danger is in thinking you know what that reason is.* Wasn't that exactly what I was thinking? But thinking of all the ways I'd let Mum down was a minefield, and I tended to avoid it.

I went to bed early that night. Whether I was a villain or not, I had an evil plan.

SIXTEEN

The overhead lights were out in Roan's room. A lone candle flickered on his dresser, dancing over his prone body. He was sprawled over his bed with his covers all akimbo, like he had wrestled himself to sleep. His back rose and fell in steady breaths.

The doctor's bag was on the floor beside him, a dark stain at the center of the room. I moved toward it. Quick. Quiet. That was the plan.

I heard a sound, like limbs hissing through the covers. I stopped. His body was still frozen in a pinwheel; his breath still thick and steady. But something had moved.

My heart rate spiked. I heard it again—the sound of something thick turning over.

The snake. Of course. I spotted the aquarium on the dresser. The snake is watching you, I thought, but that was mad.

I stepped toward the bag. All I needed to do was grab the

spell book, bring it into the hallway, find the spell, and take a few pictures on my phone and then bring it back. Easy.

I took another step. The slithering sound grew louder, but I concentrated on Roan. The snake wasn't going to stop me. The snake was in a cage. Roan wasn't.

I was close enough to see the swirling black of his tattoo, clustered at his side. It seemed to stretch, running up his back like it was alive.

I leapt back, hitting the dresser. The candle shuddered, throwing light across the black snake, running up his back. It wasn't in its cage; it was in the bed with him. He was sleeping with the snake. It lengthened, its sharp black head slipping under his shoulder, curling as it looped around his neck.

I bounded forward, grabbed its cold coil, and swept it off the bed. Roan was up in a flash, clutching a knife like some mad prisoner. I flicked the lights on. We stared at each other, breathing hard.

"What the hell are you doing?" he said, retracting the knife and collapsing back in bed.

"The snake." I scanned the rooms for signs of it. "It was out of its cage. It was going to kill you."

He set the knife down on the dresser and searched the room for the snake. I decided the best thing I could do was keep still. "Why do you keep that thing, anyway? Is it really poisonous?"

He held up a vial he wore around his neck. "Antivenom." Then he dove down and hung upside down off the end of the bed. "Aha." He stretched under the bed and dragged the snake out, artfully looped around his wrists. He hissed at it and it hissed back, darting its head and snapping its jaw.

"Jesus." I curled my lip.

Roan got up and crossed the room with it, settling it back into the aquarium. He turned to face me. "Lucky you were here." He raised his eyebrows.

"You know why I'm here."

He flicked his hair back and hopped onto the bed. "I love that you think you can just do this, like it's a card trick or something." He clucked his tongue. "You have no idea the preparation it takes, the intention, how exact every action has to be. Do you know how many people can perform a resurrection? I mean, apart from the guy everyone knows about?" He slid back on the bed so he was propped up against the wall. "I would probably let you try, solely for entertainment purposes, if I didn't care about how it would affect the Bramleys."

"I'm doing this for them."

He made a derisive snort. "Give me a break, you're not even doing this for Nikki." My chest stung, like he was tightening stitches in my heart. "Because you've asked him, right? I taught you how to do that."

"Are you saying he would rather be dead? Seventeen years old and he would rather be dead?"

"No, what I'm saying—and I think I'm being very clear—is that you don't care either way." He gripped the iron bed frame.

"I'm going to tell you a story, and I'll let you decide whether or not it's true. Once upon a time there was a boy who fell in love with another boy. This boy was like a god to him; he taught him rituals and magic. They did everything together. They used this magic as part of a performance, in an imaginary carnival called the Life and Death Parade. Their greatest performance was the Ceremony of the Black Ribbon. One boy would pretend to be dead and the other would pretend to bring him back to life. And it was wonderful and magical, like all magic is until it's real.

"One day, one of the boys died. Only this time, it wasn't pretend. And the other boy brought him back, only he wasn't pretending either. And everything was wonderful and magical, for as long as magic lasts. But then the resurrected boy came to believe he was meant to be dead. He saw signs everywhere. They drove him insane. And he killed himself, again and again. And the other boy brought him back, again and again. Until the resurrected boy set himself and everything he owned on fire. You can't resurrect ashes."

"That's horrible."

His smile unmoored me. "How is it any different from what you're asking me to do?"

"It's completely different."

"Huh." He contemplated the ceiling. "I don't really see it."

"But . . . but this is why you're here. I'm sure of it." I bit my lip.

He cocked his head. He seemed real to me in a way he never had before. Not a feline or a reptile or David Bowie—just a very sad boy. "Did you ever think I came here because I wanted to help you? I saw myself in you. I know what it's like, to want to take the world and put everything back where it belongs." He arranged his necklaces in a triangle down his chest. "Did you ever think you brought me here because you wanted to be helped?"

• • •

The next afternoon I sat alone on my chair in the library, with Nikki's empty place beside me. Around me, everyone was preparing to go to London. The Bramleys were leaving that night. They would drive to London late and spend the day there, then attend the service the following morning, on the anniversary of Nikki's death. Macklin and Roan were staying behind. As usual, I didn't know where I fit.

Holiday came in. She was wheeling her suitcase and dragging Nikki's coat. She set the coat on the footstool in front of me.

"I want you to have this," she said, stroking it like it was a living thing. "You wear your horrible army one every day."

"Cheers." She climbed onto my lap. She was nearly too big for it. She dragged the coat up with her and kept stroking it, over and over. I brushed her hair the same way.

"Are you coming to London?" She rested her head on my chest. "You can't sit next to me because I've got two friends, but you can sit next to Meghan."

I laughed. "No, I don't think so. I guess I'm not a Catholic either."

"Me neither. I told Macklin. I told him I get to be flower girl if him and Roan get married." Her brow furrowed. "Do you think Nikki would like Roan?"

"I don't know." A lump rose in my throat. "I don't know what Nikki would like anymore." I remembered the séance, which seemed ages ago now. *I love you so much more.* I swiped a tear away.

Holiday looked up at me. "Roan told me it's okay to cry. Some people think the point of life is to be happy all the time, but Roan said it's not. He said, *You're welcome to have a miserable time.*" She wiped my tears away. I smiled at her, and when I did she placed a hand on either side of my face to capture it. "I love you, Kitty," she said. She had eyes like Nikki's.

She kissed me on the nose and hopped off my lap. Then she ran from the room to her next confession. Because people like her and people like Nikki were blessed. They could say *I love you* all the time.

• • •

Lord and Lady Bramley and Holiday left for London. Roan and Macklin were nowhere to be found. I was alone in Nikki's room. I couldn't wait until after midnight, or three o'clock or anything. I needed to speak to him now.

I emptied my pockets, took off my army jacket, and put on Nikki's coat. I had set up an altar on his dresser, with all the things that once belonged to him—the notes and the stones and the journals and the jewelry. The candle fire danced uneasy. I placed Mum's card at the back of the altar.

I remembered that last morning, sitting alone with her as she slipped in and out of consciousness. How terrified I was. How I knew she was going to die, just knew, like a real psychic. A thickness permeated the air, like something was pushing, closing in on us, like the other side was forcing a hole through space to take her. Death was the worst kind of magic. It took something that was there and made it disappear.

My fingers quivered as they left the saint card. Mum watched me with her cool expression, exactly as she had done in life. I faced her for the first time since she died, knowing she wouldn't be proud of me. That she would hate my lack of direction, that she would be disappointed by my obsession with Nikki, by my refusal to move at all, by the way I had lost her and him, but mostly, by the way I had lost myself.

"I'm sorry," I said. And then I started to pray.

My fingers went numb first, then my feet. The numbness crawled in spiky veins to my brain, where the wires were reordered. I started to gasp, started to lose my breath like I was drowning, like I was crumbling into a panic attack. I saw stars.

I didn't see the sky. I saw everything; I saw nothing. I started to rock.

And then I laughed, and I gulped in my breath, and when I opened my eyes, I saw him in the mirror. Or else all I saw was myself, but I chose to see him.

"Nikki," I said. The quiet stretched long between us, the darkness in a coil. Had I completely lost it?

"Nikki," I said again. The candles juddered on the table. A gasp of smoke spat up in a line. I could feel the whole house suddenly—all the rooms and all the walls and all the people in it, like I was the place that contained it. And between the walls were echoes of things, my own memories and the echoes of memories that didn't belong to me. The spirits that lived in places beyond my mind.

"Nikki," I said. "Do you really love me more?" The altar shook.

Yes, the echo of his voice hissed, not outside me but between my ears, like an arrow.

"How can you?" Tears burned along the corners of my eyes. "I could have saved you and I didn't. So many times. All the way back. All the way back to the first day I met you, I could have saved you, but I didn't."

You did, the voice said, so quickly I thought I must have imagined it, so I waited for it to speak again.

The lights danced, the trembling became a ripple. *I didn't die because of you. I died because I had to. It was nobody's fault. It couldn't have happened any other way.*

I understood what Roan meant about death being like a cult, because even though I knew the voice belonged to Nikki, it sounded like the monotone chanting you heard in churches. It unhinged me slightly. I wanted him to be the same. I wanted him to sound the same.

"We can bring you back. Roan can."

No.

I tried to move closer to him, forgetting he wasn't anyplace. The water sloshed, and the candles flickered, and I had to steady myself, calm my racing heart.

I can't go back.

My heart stiffened. "What do you mean?"

I'm supposed to be here.

"You would rather stay there?" I almost said "without me," but I was afraid it wouldn't matter, that he didn't care.

Yes, he said so swiftly I almost didn't hear it. His words came so fast that he seemed to speak under me, as if he was responding to the thought before I said it.

"Don't you want to be with me?"

I am with you. I am with you all the time.

"But it's not the same. It's not the same as it was before."

No. It can't be.

I could feel his spirit receding. "Wait!" I gripped the dresser, so the candles shook and the water sloshed. "I have to ask you something! I have to ask you one more thing!"

But I couldn't think of anything to ask him. What did anything matter, if he wouldn't come back? The world felt very far away. The air was dense, like being underwater. Like being at the bottom of the canal. The canal, I thought. That was the question that had led me there, although I had almost forgotten it. And nothing he could say now would change anything. It was like Macklin said, understanding the past couldn't undo it. But I couldn't think of anything else to ask. "What were you so afraid of? After that night on the canal, with the psychic? What happened to you?"

I died.

I jumped in surprise and knocked the table, upsetting the altar. The bowl toppled. The candles went out. Water spread through the antique tablecloth like blood.

SEVENTEEN

Clocks ticked in the empty rooms I passed. I couldn't see them, but I could hear them, louder as I approached each open door, reaching out at me and then trickling away. I tried to call Macklin's name, but my voice sputtered, tightened my tongue. For all the empty space, I still felt watched.

Nikki's coat scraped the floor behind me. I raced along hallways, up and down stairs. I caught myself following the old tour paths, haunted by their emptiness.

I froze at the top of the grand staircase. Macklin and Roan were nowhere to be found. I needed to find someone, needed to tell someone, needed to do something. I went down the stairs in search of Edgar and Aislyn, who lived in separate quarters outside the castle. I was passing through a long hall when I noticed the open cellar door.

The Bramley cellar was a castle in itself: an airless underground castle. Rumored to have once been a crypt, it was now used to store all the priceless, useless antiques generations of

Bramleys had bought over years and years. Most of the furniture was moldy and coated in spiderwebs, run through with rats. The last time I had seen the cellar open was when it was used to store the leftover stock from the castle gift shop.

Voices rose from the ground.

"Over here?"

"No, it's over here. God, I hate rats. You should bring your snake down here."

"I do. Look, here, I found candles."

I descended into the stale air of the basement. Roan was holding out a white pillar candle with the Bramley insignia stamped on the body. Macklin was crouched over an open box. He jumped when he saw me.

I opened my mouth to speak, but I didn't know where to start. I thought I felt rats crawling over my skin, just looking at him.

Macklin glanced at Roan. "Kitty, we thought you'd gone to London."

"I decided to stay." Macklin transfixed me, the way he'd transformed in my eyes: the fancy clothes, the beautiful face, the cool customer. I moved down a step. "You lied to me."

"What are you on about?" He moved back from the box, tugged at his collar.

I steadied myself against the wall, but my fingers sank in cobwebs. I trembled, moved away. "What really happened that night?"

"What night?" He frowned.

"The night at the canal. The night Nikki died." Macklin listed, but Roan moved smoothly to his side. His arm slithered over his shoulder as he steadied him. Macklin's mouth hung open, but it didn't make a sound. His eyes were fixed on some dark point in the mazelike cellar. "Macklin, tell me or I'll think the worst."

"Don't be mean, Kitty," Roan said. "It wasn't anyone's fault. It was the cold, hard hand of fate."

"Macklin, what did you do?"

Macklin squeaked oddly. "It wasn't," he said to the floor. *"Please, Kitty."* Roan's necklaces jangled as Macklin gripped them in his hand. "I'm so sorry."

My insides plunged. I wondered what my face looked like. I couldn't imagine the type of expression a face would make, *should* make, on hearing something like that. "What happened?"

"You know how Nikki was, always taking ages to do the simplest thing. I took him to the canal so he could get his cane. I waited in the car. I waited for him for *hours.*" I remembered what Anaya said, how she and Mum's spirit spoke to Nikki for hours, convincing him that everything would be all right. How could those hours then turn against him? How could the solution be part of the problem? "I started to get annoyed. I thought I'd teach him a lesson and leave him there. I was going to come back, I thought— He could be so selfish sometimes. And I was angry with him. I wanted him to know I'd left him. I wanted him to hear the engine." He stopped.

"Macklin."

His eyelids flickered, and he squeezed Roan's necklaces so I could hear them scratch and bend together, but when he spoke his voice was deep and steady, like someone else was speaking for him. "He was dead when I got out of the car."

"What? How?"

"I hit something. I hit him."

Cold shock washed over me. I tried to keep my head level, although I felt faint. "And then?"

"I ran."

"You *ran*?" My voice was thick with disgust.

"I couldn't face it." He twitched, like a machine breaking down. "I needed to— I went to the canal and I thought about drowning. I thought about . . . I prayed for a miracle. I honestly did," he said like I should thank him for it. His eyes met mine, and his voice whispered, "How could I have known it was going to happen?"

"A psychic did warn us hours before," I snapped. I knew I wasn't helping the situation, but I couldn't stop myself; I was shocked, shocked and furious and, frankly, terrified. I had never, ever thought . . . Macklin had killed Nikki. If it weren't for him, none of this would have happened. If it weren't for him, Nikki would still be here. And all this time, I had blamed myself. "You never said anything. You lied."

"I thought it wasn't real. It was like a dream."

"Every real thing is like a dream," I said. "That's how you know it's real."

"I went back." He steadied himself enough to step toward me. The blue moonlight coming down from the cellar door rolled over him. "I went back to face it, but he was there, just like he was before, like nothing had happened. I thought I was going mad. What would you have done?"

"I would like to think I would have done more. When Nikki was going mad, you did nothing." He flinched. "You hardly ever spoke to him. You just went racing around in the car you used to run him down." Macklin's dark hair hung over his face. His features were becoming indistinct to me; he was becoming more and more like some wraith drawn from a nightmare.

Roan stepped forward. "If I could just fill in what he left out, because that was kind of my moment. Macklin prayed for a miracle, and me being a hero of this life and the next, I gave him one."

"You brought Nikki back," I said. "So you knew each other all this time? You'd met before."

"No," Macklin said. "I didn't see him that night. He only just told me."

"It was a random act of resurrection," Roan explained.

"Why?"

"For Macklin. Of course."

I sat down on the steps. I ran my thumb along the stone,

along the spaces in between, where everything was held together. "Is that why you're down here? Is this what you're doing, bringing him back again?"

"That's the idea."

"But you told me no. You said you wouldn't do it."

"We wanted to surprise you," Macklin said.

"And anyway, when you're performing real magic, the last thing you want is a crowd." Roan shrugged.

"So that's your solution? You bring Nikki back and he stalks around the castle, wishing he were dead. How long do you think it will last this time?" I shook my head. "Only the dead can live in the past."

"Can't you understand, Kitty?" Macklin said, his voice rough with pleading. "If he's dead, then I killed him."

I did understand. I understood exactly, but somehow that made me angrier. "You did kill him," I said. "It doesn't matter what you bring back. You can't change what happened."

"Then what is the future for?" Macklin said, elbowing away from Roan. "What is living for, if you can make a mistake that lasts forever? If I bring him back, then it's not my fault." His eyes ran along the lines of my face, searching for something, searching for an answer he could live with.

I couldn't face him, so I turned to Roan. I remembered the story he'd told me, about the two boys, and the boy he'd loved and resurrected. Emmanuel. "You of all people should know better. You watched Emmanuel kill himself over and over and you kept on, even when you knew he didn't want it. That's not love."

"I know it isn't." The flames tattooed on Roan's torso caught the candlelight so they seemed to be burning, a fire stitched to his side.

I lifted myself to my feet, still weak at the knees. "I have to get out of here."

"Kitty, please," Macklin said.

I knew this was the part where I was supposed to forgive him, but I couldn't. Macklin had killed Nikki. He had lied to everyone.

"I can't stay here," I said. "I can't stay here with you."

• • •

I walked up from the cellar, past the silent automatons, the birds twittering in the aviary. I kept walking until I was outside, choking on the fresh air. Darkness covered the sky like a cloak, with little holes poked through where light dripped out.

I went to the garage. Macklin's car gleamed with an almost maniacal purity. I tried to find the seam, where it had been repaired after the accident, but it was hauntingly perfect and put together, just like he was.

I saw in a flash that night: Macklin waiting in his car, Nikki on the boat, trying to charm his way out of fate. The way it all came together in a horrible spectacle—a performance for no one, with the kind of gags only Greek gods would get.

I didn't want to be part of the show anymore. I wanted out.

I took the keys to one of Lord Bramley's Jags. I pulled out of the garage. As I was curving along the circular drive, I noticed a dark figure sitting on the edge of the fountain, underneath the arc of the stone snake. It stood and walked slowly to the center of the road, blocking me in. I slowed to a stop.

Roan walked around the side of the car. His necklaces clinked joyfully. He set his hands on either side of the window.

"What do you want?" I said.

"I just wanted to make sure you're okay, that's all."

"I don't understand you." I shook my head.

"Kitty." He leaned into the car, folding his arms along the windowsill and tilting his head almost dreamily. "You of all people should understand. There are the things they give you and the things they take from you, and every year—no, every hour—their list gets longer." He shifted closer to me. "And no matter how hard you play, they always win. They take everything. Not only the things you love but the people, the moments. They take your mind. They take your life. So why shouldn't we play dirty? Why shouldn't we fight hard? Why shouldn't we take something, take everything we can, back?" I gripped the steering wheel but trained my eyes on the road ahead of me. I did understand him, and he knew it.

"I did what you said. I asked Nikki. He doesn't want to come back."

"He didn't want to die either." His words moved stealthily

over me. "Maybe he's accepted it now, but that's only because he's dead." His words tightened the air. "Death doesn't just take from the living; it takes from the dead, too. If you brought him back, he would be himself again—angry and afraid and maybe a little bit dangerous, but alive. Isn't that the most important thing?"

"And what about the Bramleys? What do you think they'll say?"

He ran a finger along the windowsill. "Thank you very much."

I shuddered. "There's something monstrous about you."

"Maybe." He stood back, his jewelry forming an arrow over his heart. "But isn't there something monstrous about God? What's the difference between Him and me? Both of us just take what we want, because we can."

"You're wrong," I said.

"There is no right and wrong." His teeth flashed. "There's only life and death."

• • •

As soon as the castle disappeared from my rearview mirror, I felt myself deflating. Where was I going? I had nowhere to go to.

My hands shook as I pulled to the side of the road. I killed the engine. I released the steering wheel. And suddenly I had a date with a destination: the past.

That night flooded over me, in fairy lights strung up and

down the Hartfords' garden, a limp fortress against the dark. Tottering along the towpath in those uncomfortable shoes, that constricting dress. And Nikki standing beside me with his cane. *Will you come with me? To tell you the truth, I'm sort of scared to go alone.*

But I wasn't there, and he did go alone, and I didn't know whether it was Macklin or myself that I couldn't forgive. Because I should have known.

My words to Macklin came thundering back: *A psychic did warn us hours before.* That was what I most regretted. That I didn't believe when I should have. I never believed that Nikki could die.

And I still didn't believe it. I had kept everything exactly the same, had stayed in a world that only made sense with Nikki there. I was waiting for him. I had left him a space, fought for and protected it, as the old world started crumbling over my head.

I squeezed the steering wheel, spun it toward the castle even though the engine was dead. I wanted to go home. I wanted to bring Nikki back. Maybe Roan was right; maybe Nikki would come around. I tried to remember him as he was after the accident—it wasn't all bad, was it? And I would help him. I would believe in him. I could fix him, I was sure of it. I could make everything right, if only I had another chance.

I let myself imagine what it would be like to wake up next

to Nikki, to hide out all day in bed, under the covers, to go out and play in the sun. It would be like the world of my past and the world of my dreams combined, and wasn't that what heaven was supposed to be? Wasn't that the ending I deserved?

I took the two cards from the two sides of my coat and propped them on the dashboard in front of me. Placed side by side, I could really see the differences between them: Roan active, fighting, almost frightening, and Mum serene, at peace, oddly comforting.

I could let Roan bring Nikki back, prop up the old world before it buried me, or I could do what Nikki wanted me to do and stop them, but to do that I would have to step out into a new world, a world filled with nothing—no castle, no family, no past.

My eyes caught on Mum's card and I could almost hear her say, *That's not true.* I didn't have nothing. I had whatever I believed in.

The one thing I'd learned was that there was no place to go and find faith: I couldn't walk into a church, see it in a séance, drink it in tea, or dance it free at a party. It was always and only my choice. It only works if you believe it.

I pulled my mobile out of my pocket. It felt strange for me to dial, strange to ask someone else for help, but it was a good sort of strange.

"Hello?"

"Hey, Joy. This is Kitty."

"Oh, I hoped you'd call! Do you want to come over? I got this really amazing new tea, it's not magical or anything, but it tastes like heaven—the place, not the drink."

"Actually, I need your help. I need to find the Life and Death Parade."

EIGHTEEN

I trudged through mud and mist toward the camp. It had taken all night and well into the morning to track down the Life and Death Parade. I tried to keep calm by reminding myself that the actual anniversary wasn't until three o'clock tonight, but I couldn't stop feeling that something bad might happen at any moment. I needed to get back to the castle.

I hurried along the camp's perimeter, toward the canal. A performer, his face smeared with the previous night's paint, puffed a rolled cigarette from the back of a cluttered carriage. Safi stacked coffins in the bed of his coach. The smoke of dying fires carried the smell of fresh coffee and stale tobacco. The boats along the canal looked half-awake, strung like dead fish along the water.

I spotted Anaya's boat at the head of the lineup. The engine hummed to life, and Anaya appeared at the back. She was about to leave her mooring. I abandoned the perimeter and ran straight through the camp, dodging spirit bottles and bottles of spirits. The boat slipped out onto the water.

"Wait!" I shouted, waving my arms as I reached the towpath. She scowled when she saw me. "I need to talk to you!" She turned away. I ran along the towpath until the boat was just beside me.

"What do you want?" she demanded. I didn't have the breath to answer her. I made a running start and leapt onto the front deck.

I caught myself on the railing, held steady as the boat thrummed beneath me. Once I had gotten my bearings, I moved onto the deck and through the door. This time I remembered the step down. I heard Anaya banging through the doors at the opposite end of the boat.

The floor rocked as the boat skidded along the side of the canal. Anaya appeared inside the door, hair wild.

"Shouldn't you be steering?" I gasped as we knocked against the shore. A mess of objects—stones and crystals, prescription drugs and FINAL NOTICE bills—tumbled in a waterfall from the shelves and cupboards and flooded the floor.

Anaya threw her hands up. "Fate can take the wheel."

The boat pitched. I found myself sprawled across the table. "It doesn't seem to be doing a very good job," I said.

"What is it you want?" She stood with her feet wide apart to steady her, placed her hands on her hips, and raised an eyebrow. "Have you come to shout at me again?"

I forced myself up. "I want to speak to my mother."

The boat quaked. Anaya caught herself on the altar. "Ah. Now we're talking."

. . .

Anaya moored the boat on the side of the canal as the other boats sailed past. "We don't have much time," she said, setting up a shrine from the pieces scattered across the floor.

I bent down to help her.

"Don't touch anything!" I put both hands in the air. "Sorry," she said. "But these things are very special to me." She scooped up a pile of old bills and pills, and dumped them on the counter. Then she looked at me properly for the first time.

She moved toward me quickly, slid her hand along the back of my neck. "Where did you get this coat?"

"Nikki. Nikki used to wear it all the time. Why?"

"It's . . ." Her hands shook as she turned out the back collar, then ran her fingers along the lapel, down the skull-imprinted buttons. "This is my son's."

"Your son?"

She stepped back fast. "Emmanuel." She glared at me, eyebrows descending.

"*Emmanuel* is your son?"

Her eyebrows dipped. "What do you know about Emmanuel?"

"Nothing. I know Roan."

She shrank away from me. "He sent you."

"No, of course not. Why would he send me? Here, I'm sorry about the coat." I slipped it from my shoulders. "Take it." I held it out to her and then pulled it back, remembering. "Wait." I tried to remove the cards from either pocket so she wouldn't see, but she snatched them both from my fingers.

Her eyebrows darted up her forehead. "Why do you have this card?" She lifted the picture of Roan like it was an indictment. She backed away from me.

"I bought it."

She flung the cards at me. "You need to leave." She snatched the coat from my hands. "He sent you here, didn't he? Tell me." She backed through the boat, wading through the junk on the floor.

I slid the cards into my back pockets and held up my hands. "No, no. He doesn't even know that I'm here!"

"I had a feeling. You have a dark shadow over you," she said.

I moved toward her. "Anaya, listen to me. I'm here to stop him—that's why I'm here."

She glanced down at her shaking hands, discordant, like she had been given someone else's hands by mistake. "That monster killed my son."

"*He* did?" He'd never mentioned that.

Her eyes found mine. They were wide, rimmed with wet. "He thought he was invincible." She grabbed and squeezed my hand, suddenly, like I had to understand. "The snake. It was his idea to start using a poisonous snake, like they did in the real rituals.

He wore antivenom in a vial around his neck." She clutched at her throat. "It had to be real, he said. It had to be as close to real as possible." She laughed once abruptly. "I sometimes think that irony is the most powerful force in the universe."

"The snake bit Emmanuel?"

"It bit them both." He eyebrows twitched. "Who do you think got the antivenom?" She stumbled toward her altar, laid the coat beside it like a body, ran her fingers down the fabric. "That boy. He condemned my son to hell. Every day, I try to contact Emmanuel. Even your mother can't bring him to me. He's lost, forever." She poured water from the tap into a filmy crystal bowl and set in on the altar. "Come, then." She flicked at her eyes. "Enough of this, let's get started."

I felt sick for her. Was there really a place you could go where even the dead couldn't contact you? And what if the same thing happened to Nikki? What if he ended up trapped in some sort of hell?

I put my hand on her shoulder. "I'm so sorry," I said.

She put her hand over mine, eyes still on the altar, and squeezed my fingers. "I have faith."

I went to sit at the table of snakes. I traced them with my finger; I wondered what they meant; good or evil, life or death, nothing or everything. They seemed to twist on the table as my finger ran round and round. Anaya prayed. The air grew thick and then thin. The candles quivered in time. The ground dropped and lifted. My fingers and toes and lips went numb.

"She's here," Anaya intoned. "She's very unhappy about your hair."

I laughed in spite of myself. "Does she like the piercing?"

"She's telling you to watch it." I heard Mum's tone in Anaya's voice. Like it was just another day, in another world, and all of us were sitting down to tea. I felt the love that still ran between us fully, for the first time since she died.

Anaya went quiet, bent forward as if she was straining to hear. "She wanted to tell you that she's sorry. She left the Life and Death Parade for you. She saw death in your future and wanted to save you from it. What she learned is that you can't fight fate. Or your fight becomes fate. What is meant to happen will happen."

All that was well and good, but I was after something more specific. I stopped tracing the snakes. "Tell her I need her help."

"She knows what you need," Anaya scolded.

"I need to stop Roan." I crouched forward in my seat, fists on the table. "Ask her how I can stop Roan."

Anaya went still. With her head bowed, her back was like a tower of scarves. It heaved as she breathed in deeply. "She says you can't."

The chair toppled over behind me as I sprung to my feet. "What?"

"She says you can't stop Roan. You can't stop evil from entering your life. It is part of your destiny. It is part of your life, yours and everyone's."

"That's ridiculous." I dug my fingernails into my palms, ready to fight. "I need to stop him."

"She says no. You can't stop him. His powers will go on and on. Powers like his are eternal."

I shook my head. "So I'm supposed to do nothing?"

"She says have faith."

I stomped my foot like a child. "That's not enough."

"That's all there is."

• • •

The last of the carriages were pulling out of camp as I stormed through the field, going nowhere, to do nothing. I paused to let them pass, a string of cheap tricks and broken dreams. Have faith? I did have faith, and it was definitely not enough.

I couldn't help being slightly dubious of Anaya, hoarding all that junk, letting the debris of her past bury her alive. Even though she blamed Roan for her son's death, she'd never thought to confront him; she'd never even tried to stop him. She'd looked relieved to see me go, so she could close herself inside her boat, door shutting like the lid of a coffin.

I stopped in my tracks. Coffin. I scanned the fields as the last of the carriages rattled off. I spotted the flat back of Safi's carriage, the coffins rollicking together beneath their ties. I gathered myself and ran again. I called out to him, but that only seemed to make him move faster. I raced across the emptying fields until I reached his carriage. I grabbed a coffin by the handle and swung myself on board.

"Oi!" Safi shouted back at me. "What you doing?" He flicked his whip and the horses went faster. The carriage jounced, and I caught myself around a casket. Determined, I slithered up the coffins until I reached the seat beside him. "Look, mate, show's over." He tilted up his black top hat. "Ah, wait a tick. You're a mate of Roan's, innit?"

"How do you stop a resurrection?"

"Yep." His teeth glimmered. "Definitely a mate of Roan's." He pulled at the reins so the carriage slowed, but not by much. "It's not real, eh? It's all a show. What he does is—"

"I know it's real. He brought back a friend of mine."

Safi shook his head wearily, like I wasn't the first person to be taken in by Roan. "Never happened."

"Yes. It did."

Safi was unmoved. "No. He wouldn't do it. He doesn't do things for other people; it's not in his nature."

"He is doing it. He's doing it for Macklin. He's in love with him."

"What, that posh boy from the party?" He snorted. "No chance. Roan is not in love with that boy. I've known Roan a *long* time. He'll never stop loving Emmanuel; he can't. They don't make saints out of people who change their minds."

"But they—" The words soured on my tongue. If Roan didn't love Macklin, none of this made sense. Why would he bring Nikki back? Why had he told me he wouldn't? Why would he try to teach me some grand lesson about moving on, if he were planning to bring Nikki back anyway? And the whole setup was unnerving: just him and Macklin bringing Nikki back, alone.

But Roan *had* brought Nikki back before. I'd seen the after-effects. Macklin had confessed to killing him. Why would Roan have done that? He didn't seem the type to pass out random acts of resurrection.

Anaya had said, *Every day, I try to contact Emmanuel.* But if Emmanuel was dead, why couldn't Anaya speak to him?

And why had Nikki worn that coat every single day, when it didn't even belong to him?

I groped for the seat as the carriage lurched beneath me. "Could he use another body?"

"What?" Safi steadied the horses.

"Roan, to bring Emmanuel back. Does it have to be Emmanuel's body?"

He laughed. "It doesn't even have to be a human body. Why do you think he carts that snake around?"

NINETEEN

My excursion to the Life and Death Parade had taken me hours away from the castle. On the way back, in between planning my attack, I tried to get my head around Emmanuel-as-Nikki. There were little things that made sense now—the way he smelled, the way he said things like *Love is a scary thing* and *If I told you, you'd make me leave* and the journals he had studied to play the part. But it was too much to comprehend—Nikki being someone else as himself—and anyway it was in the past. My future was in danger.

When the castle finally appeared, it looked like something from a dream: stone-cold and fixed, so far away I could never reach it. A backhoe curled like a question mark over the cemetery. The statue at the center of the fountain seemed to move as I spun around it: Adam and Eve wrestling the snake.

I parked the car at the bottom of the steps. As I marched up them, the castle reared away from me. I stopped to stare into the stone, like the walls of a sarcophagus, thousands of years old. And then I took another step, and another step, until I was inside it.

The statues were under their drop cloths and the lights were out everywhere, so I thought maybe I'd missed it—not just by minutes or moments but by ten or two hundred thousand years. It was possible, in a place like this, to stop time.

I knew exactly where I would find them. I knew because Anaya and the serpent spirit had told me my future at the LDP party. *He's showing me a church filled with books. That's where it happens. That's where he dies.* And the last part, the part I thought was about Nikki and me: *The one he loves kills him.* Roan was going to kill Macklin and use his body to bring Emmanuel back.

I had to be smart. I couldn't let Roan read me this time. I couldn't let him know what I knew. I also couldn't go in empty-handed. The weapons room had been put on lockdown after Nikki, but there had to be something, somewhere.

I remembered Nikki's sword, now blessed and mounted over Holiday's bedroom door. I went there first, stood on a chair, and lifted it from the wall. I had no coat to cover it, so I went to Mum's room and found my army jacket. I strapped the sword to my side, over my shirt and under my jacket. It was partly visible from the back, and it nipped my flesh when I moved too fast, but it would have to do.

A funny barnyard smell permeated the main hallway leading up to the library. I realized what it was when I dodged a patch of manure. Horses. Perfect for an apocalypse. I paused outside the library doors to adjust the sword. Then I took a deep breath and soldiered in.

The chapel was awash with trembling lights, edging the shelves, down spiraled iron staircases, on ladders and along the floor. There were four harnessed horses tethered in the corner of the room—two white to purify and two black to send it back—and a rusted carriage they must have used to carry Nikki's coffin. The coffin rested now in nearly the exact place his body had fallen that night. Earth still clung to it, adorned with long strands of yellowing roots.

The Bramleys had bought the most expensive coffin money could buy—painted with a painstaking replica of the mural on the chapel ceiling, down to the gold leafing. The coffin seemed to belong there beneath its origin story, the guest of honor at a second funeral.

Macklin stood by the fireplace, which was as great and billowing as it had been that night. Roan stood beside him. He reached up with a brooding intensity and pushed a strand of black hair behind Macklin's ear.

"I thought you'd gone," Roan said in a tone that told me I was on my way out.

"I'm not staying," I said, willing him to believe me. I kept my face a mask, like he did, affecting the coolness, the professionalism, like life was a game rigged for my amusement. Roan narrowed his eyes. A hunk of earth dropped from the coffin to the floor. "I wanted to say something to Macklin."

Macklin's eyes darted up, wholly pleading. Anger coursed through me. How could I not blame him for what happened to Nikki? He was driving. And he lied, to all of us. I wanted to punish him, tear him down the way I'd torn myself down.

But where would that blaming lead? It wasn't about me. It wasn't even about what I believed. It was about being able to live with something horrible, a mistake that lasted forever. And the only way to live with something that bad was to lie—no, not to lie, but to choose a truth that could transform the past and give us a new future.

"Macklin." I held his gaze, and I saw in his eyes the boy I grew up with—the boy we grew up with, Nikki and me. Always vaguely annoying but somehow perfect, somehow ours. "It's not your fault. People die, everywhere and all the time. You didn't invent the world. You aren't the god who takes them. And Nikki forgives you. I spoke to him, and he said it was nobody's fault. He said it couldn't have happened any other way." I gathered myself, struggling to keep my face a mask, to keep the sword a secret, to keep my steps even. I spread open my arms. He came toward me. I watched Roan's hand reach out to grab him, but he moved too late and it dropped in the empty air.

I wrapped my arms around Macklin. I brushed my fingers through his hair as Roan watched, his face a picture of peace.

Macklin sobbed into my shoulder. My heart sprang loose, and I gasped. Roan's lip twitched, and he winked.

I tightened my grip on Macklin, spun him toward the door, and hissed hotly in his ear, "I need you to trust me when I tell you to *run and hide*." My back was to Roan, but I felt him slip closer to me, the cold sweep of a bad thing. "Go!" I screamed, shoving Macklin toward the door. And he trusted me, and he ran.

I unsheathed the sword from my side, fingers slick with sweat, and pointed it at Roan. He pulled up short in front of me. He watched Macklin vanish with that chilly expression, like he was a quick calculation short of total world domination.

His eyes fell on me. His lip curved. He took a step forward.

I shook the sword. "Stop where you are. I will kill you."

He put both hands up, then walked in an arc away from me. I scanned the room, to see if he was trying for a weapon. One of the horses stamped its foot, and I nearly dropped the sword. Roan raised an eyebrow at me, then collapsed coolly into Nikki's chair and put his feet up, crossed at the ankle. Beside him, the coffin glowed as if alive. "I thought you wanted Macklin and me to be together." He shook his head. "You really need to make up your mind."

"I know exactly what you're planning to do." I should have stabbed him. I knew that. That was the mistake all good guys made, not to fillet the bad guy at the first opportunity. But bad guys never seemed bad in real life, or not *all* bad. They seemed like people you knew, people you liked. And—worst of all—people you understood. "That wasn't Nikki you brought back. That wasn't Nikki at all."

"Don't be so dramatic." He stuck a finger between his lips and bit the tip of his nail off, then spat it onto the floor. "It was *his* corpse." His entire posture had changed, like a snake that had shed its skin. I could see what was pulsing underneath—the one thing he wanted, the one thing he would do anything to get.

I aimed the sword at him, fingers throbbing with rage and fear. "Why Nikki?"

"Come over here and I'll tell you." He jerked his head and grinned at me, like it was all a joke. Then he slid down on the chair, like he was settling in. "Do you ever get the feeling that things have come together almost too perfectly? So perfectly that it seems like they were meant to happen?" he spat. "Do you ever get that feeling, Kitty? I had that feeling once. After Emmanuel burned himself alive at the Life and Death Parade.

"He burned himself and everything that belonged to him—everything we had. Objects have a kind of power, in ritual work." He ran his fingers through his necklaces. "I needed something that belonged to him, to anchor me, so I could bring him back again. I also needed a body. So I went to Anaya's boat to steal Emmanuel's coat, and what did I find but Anaya convincing Nikki it was okay to die young and leave a good-looking corpse. And that wasn't all; I had met Nikki before. I made him a love spell at Emmanuel's funeral. So when I saw him spattered on the road, I did what any aspiring god would do: I used your tragedy for my own ends. I brought Emmanuel back. Then just as he was waking up, I heard someone coming and I hid."

He observed his fingernails. "You know, I think I fell in love with Macklin at first sight. I fell in love with his body. I also realized I was in for a lot of paperwork, so I let him take Emmanuel back here." His eyes drifted over the mural on the ceiling and he scowled. "Emmanuel stayed with you longer than I would have guessed, but I knew he wouldn't be able to live without me—*I keep him alive.*" I remembered what Emmanuel-as-Nikki was like: superstitious, afraid, and obsessed with ending his curse. I wondered if he stayed so long because he knew there was no escape for him.

"I learned my lesson," Roan continued. "Don't resurrect people willy-nilly. Even if they fall onto your plate, nothing is meant to be. You have to fight for what you want. So if you want to steal someone's body, make friends first. Get to know their family. If you can get them to love you, even better." He slid lower in his chair. "And it's all thanks to you, Kitty. You brought Macklin to me." He slid still farther. "If that's not fate, then I don't know what is."

"You don't believe in fate."

"No. But you do." He fell flat on the chair, stretched his arm down behind it. And then something flew through the air toward me, glinting like a mirror. I felt it sink deep beneath my collarbone. The sword dropped from my hand, clattered on the floor.

Roan was out of his chair and then he was there, and the sword was at my throat, and his hand was on the knife, twisting it inside me. I cried out. "I really like you, Kitty."

"I'm finding that hard to believe"—I grunted—"at the moment." I was impressed with my ready wit. Everything had sharpened on the blade of the knife. I might be about to die. And suddenly the world seemed rife with humor.

"I'm not the bad guy here." He slid the knife out, and I staggered back. It hurt more out than it did in. I pressed my hand hard against the wound as blood trickled in a pulse.

"Again," I said. "There are believability issues."

His eyes blazed in the candlelight. "Emmanuel died for no reason, same as Nikki. All I'm trying to do is put the reason back."

"By killing somebody else?"

"At least I have a reason. God doesn't."

"*God,*" I exhaled, feeling light-headed. All of this was wildly surreal. Like magic. I moved carefully away from him, searching for something to put between us. The vestry door hung open, and I staggered toward it. "Emmanuel gave you the antivenom, didn't he?" I gulped in panicked gasps. "He wanted you to live. He died for you."

He shook his head. "We decided, together. He knew I could use the ritual to bring him back. It was so close to real already;

all we needed was a reason to believe it." He bristled. "But then he died and he changed. Suddenly he didn't want to come back. He was like one of you, accepting his fate, even though it happened for nothing and no one. All I want is to have Emmanuel back to what he was before."

"But you can't." My back was against the wall, and I slid very slowly along it toward the vestry door. "You can't own a person, you can't keep a memory. Everything in this life is temporary. It will never be the same again."

He shrugged. "I would settle for better."

The wall ended and I let myself fall back into the vestry. Roan darted toward me, sword poised. I rolled on the floor and kicked the door shut as he reached it, then leapt to my feet and slammed the lock.

• • •

It didn't take long to realize what a stupid plan this was. I was trapped in the vestry with no way out, and nothing but flimsy lattice screens between us.

He rattled the door. "What are you doing in there?" Good question.

The candle I'd used to burn the letter from school was still on the prayer altar. Mum had told me to have faith. I wasn't sure how helpful it would be, but I absolutely believed I was going to die.

I picked up a book of matches and lit the candle. I had a

glass but no water. Luckily, I was really starting to bleed now, so I dripped the blood into a bowl. With a wild ripping sound, the sword plunged through the lattice, crossing inches from my nose.

"Are you actually building an altar?" He peered in through the hole he'd made in the lattice. "Who do you think is going to help you now?"

I pulled his card from my pocket and held it flat against the window. "You are."

He startled, dropping back. "Where did you get that?"

"The Life and Death Parade."

"Let me see!" he said, his voice suddenly young. "What powers did they give me?" His fingers reached through the lattice.

I pulled the card back and read out, "Resurrection, youth, obsession. Also, mercy," I added, but he snorted in disbelief. Then he dropped from behind the lattice.

I took a deep breath, forcing myself to concentrate. I placed the card at the head of the altar. I shut my eyes and began to chant. I felt a heady, airy lightness, almost transcendent, and then the door came crashing in.

The blood spilled. The candle toppled, catching on the rug. I needed to put the flames out, but I had bigger problems.

Roan caught me, swung me around, and slammed me against the wall. He had his hands around my neck. I felt them tighten with a strange detachment, a cool professionalism. The flames jumped as his jeans caught fire, but it only seemed to enrage him. He crushed me hard against the wall and kicked his leg against it, to put the fire out.

"You lack conviction," he spat. "You wait for the world to work things out for you; what you don't realize is that the world doesn't care about you. The world breaks your heart, but your heart is nothing to the world." I felt my own heart flutter, like an automaton winding down. "The world can't even feel it." My vision speckled around the edges. I thought I was going to faint. I knew I was going to die. I tried to see past Roan, into the library, where Nikki was, tried to tell him I would be with him soon.

My vision split, like the two sides of the world had cracked open. And I saw Macklin. I fluttered my eyes in disbelief. The snake was on his shoulders, like a black cloud, and he met my eyes and shouted, "Stop." Roan's fingers slackened. The world came trickling in. "Let her go. You can have me, if you let her go."

Roan turned to watch him, but his grip on me tightened. Macklin ran his hand along the snake. I saw it, dizzy, drawn from a fever dream, a death dream. He took its head, pushed apart its jaw. The snake hissed as Macklin forced its fangs down on his snow-white neck.

Macklin blinked prettily, as if half in a trance. "How long does it take to—" His arm dropped. He staggered and collapsed.

Roan hissed. His fingers contracted, then loosened. I gasped, groping at my throat as he moved away from me.

Roan strode to Macklin's fallen body as the snake slid toward him. The fire in the vestry had gone out, but it had mangled the flesh all the way up Roan's side. His tattoo was a charred mess of ink. He paused to scoop up the sword. The snake slithered between his legs, then seemed to urge him forward.

I wheezed against the wall, unable to catch my breath. I needed to get the antivenom, to save Macklin, but how could I? It was around Roan's neck. Have faith, I thought stupidly. I scanned the room for something, some weapon to contain him, but I had nothing, nothing to believe in. Roan crouched down over Macklin's body as the snake slithered up his leg.

The serpent spirit was wrong. The one he loved didn't kill Macklin. Macklin had killed himself. Unless . . .

The snake was climbing now, scaling Roan's side, crossing like a black arrow over his heart. I staggered forward, watched the snake as it curved over Roan's shoulder. Roan had his fingers pressed to Macklin's wrist. He turned his head as I collapsed beside him. My fingers fumbled, groped the curve of the snake, and pulled it tight around Roan's neck.

The snake obliged me, tightening the noose. The sword dropped to the floor. Roan's arms flailed, trying to grab me as I skated back away from him. And the snake contracted, tighter and tighter. Until Roan's face went blue. Until his eyes went red. Until he rattled, stiffened, and fell to the floor.

The snake released him, slithering along the floor. I pounced on Roan's body, clawing through the necklaces, searching for the antivenom.

"Where is it?" I called after the snake, but it raced off away from me, fleeing the scene. Roan's body was still warm. His necklaces jingled between my fingers.

"What are you doing?" Macklin was sitting up across from me. I flew back from the body, heart racing.

"The antivenom." I gasped. "You're—"

He smiled lightly. "It wasn't real, Kitty. It was all just a trick."

I pressed my palm to my pounding heart, to reassure myself I was alive. My eyes followed the light of the flames to the ceiling where a heavenly mural spun. Angels being dragged to hell—but exquisitely—like death was a beautiful, magical thing.

Now trouble has gone,
Dissolved in this song,
Ah drink from my cup
We'll make it all up.
You don't have to switch when you see
the lights flicker,
Down the long hallway,
There lies a brand new day.

—Alan Wass, "I'm at Ease with You"

TWENTY

The End of Summer party was a fairy-lit affair in the back garden of the Bramley Castle. I was in my bedroom, lighting candles. I wasn't asking for anything. I was saying thank you.

I understood now that there was a vein of magic running through everything, the way the Life and Death Parade ran through hidden hills. It was there if you went looking. It was real if you believed it. You couldn't find answers, but you could find meaning, if you wanted to.

I stepped back as Macklin came in. He was dressed in black and white, perfectly put together. "You all right?" he said.

"Yeah, I'm just saying thanks," I said, which made me feel slightly cheesy. It was easy to pray, but it was pretty much impossible to talk about praying.

"Can you say thanks for me, too?" he said, sitting on a chair across from me. It had been months since the night of the attempted resurrection, but Macklin's face told a troubled story. Still, I thought it was better than no story at all.

The cards I had collected over the past few months were on the table. Macklin picked them up and flicked through the deck. I had been back to the Life and Death Parade a few times with Joy, but Macklin never wanted to come. He frowned at the cards. "There are a lot of messed-up-looking people in here."

"Messed-up people are the best people." I grinned my best messed-up grin.

He flicked to the next card and inhaled sharply. "You kept it."

"Yeah." I tried to shrug but couldn't. "It happened. We'll never understand *why*, but I don't want to pretend it never happened." I wasn't sure of what I was saying, but Macklin nodded like he understood. "Besides," I continued, "you never know, I might need it one day." My back bristled at the possibility.

He ran a finger over the card and exhaled carefully, parceling it out. His eyes caught the candlelight and burned green. "Can I have it?"

I hesitated. "Okay." He opened his jacket and tucked it in his breast pocket. I bit my lip. "Were you really in love with him?"

"I don't know," he said, carefully re-buttoning his jacket. "There's something romantic about people you can't have."

"You can never *have* anyone, but you can love them." I offered him a hopeless smile.

I knew what love was now. Love was the best thing to believe in.

Macklin stood up, fussing with his collar. "Are you going?"

My mind was lagging, so I shook my head, confused. "Where?"

"To the party."

"No." I paused, fingered the long matches down on the table. "We should just go."

"Pardon?"

Another messed-up grin spread across my face. "Let's just go." I took his hand. It didn't feel foreign or strange anymore. It was like taking my own hand. I started to move, quickly, out of the room, down the hall.

Macklin laughed in surprise but fell into step beside me. "Where will we go?"

"Does it matter?" I could see through the window, Lord and Lady Bramley at the party; Holiday running in a pack with her friends. I reached for the door. "The point is, we don't have to stay here."

ACKNOWLEDGMENTS

At the beginning of this novel is an excerpt from the last poem my husband wrote, after the first time he died, with his arm in a sling, unable to move his fingers, so it was barely legible. That is what writers do. We write through pain, we write until the end, and when the end comes we hope there will be someone to pick up where we left off.

Thank you to Emily Meehan and Hannah Allaman for tireless work and incredible patience.

Thank you to my agent Madeleine Milburn for supporting me through difficult times.

Thank you to Sarah White for fresh eyes on short notice.

Thank you to Kiersten White for helping me navigate the publishing world and Elena Hecht for helping me navigate the bereavement world.

Thank you to Janelle, Emmanuel, "Alfred," and all those who have supported and guided me. You are the real magic.